The Meerkat Murders

The Meerkat Murders

R. J. Corgan

2019

Art by Justus Lyons

Tree image credit: Diego Delso, License CC-BY-SA

Meerkat image credit: Charlesjsharp (Wikimedia)

First Printing: 2019

ISBN: 978-0-359-63400-2

www.RJCorganBooks.com

Other books in the Kea Wright series:

Cold Flood

For my father.
A good man
who tells terrible jokes.

Chapter 1 - Meerkat Yoga

HEAD OVER heart.

Heart over hips.

As the sun simmered just beneath the horizon, soft hues of orange and yellow seeped up into the twilight, obscuring the remaining stars that freckled the sky.

Kea Wright sat cross-legged on the frigid sands, shivering within a blanket. Her diminutive figure was hidden within the twisted roots of a baobab tree. Its twisted, bulbous bulk loomed over her, threatening to overwhelm her with its sheer mass. The tree didn't belong here. Clawing for purchase within a ridge of exposed rock, its limbs were twisted and stunted as its tendrils squeezed their way into the unforgiving strata, desperate to fit in.

She knew how it felt.

Kea's normally clear brown eyes were surrounded by dark, sullen bags, her lids red with exhaustion. Stray strands of ginger hair poked out from beneath the rim of her hat, their ends split and frayed. Her ruddy cheeks and snub nose were coated with grit, her lips cracked and peeling. The last year had taken a toll that she hadn't had any desire to disguise. Not that she ever cared about her appearance. She had become a geologist in order to connect to the planet and wore her sun-blessed wrinkles as badges of honor. Lately, however, her passion for her work, and for life in general, had withered. Buying lip balm seemed frivolous. Pointless.

It doesn't matter. Nothing matters.

Kea shook her head and tried to empty her mind.

Breathe out.

As the sun began to bake the air into shimmering waves, she felt the last chill of the night rush away, skimming her cheeks.

Think of nothing.

Unbidden, a memory of terror raked across her soul. She remembered the grip of her attacker's hands on her legs, of kicking him again and again, until he was swept away by a wall of boulders and ice that roiled toward her, threatening to smother her.

"Think of nothing," she repeated aloud to calm herself.

1

Head over heart.
Heart over hips.
Breathe in.

Delicate streamers of clouds, hidden by the dark cloak of night, were teased into shape by the morning sun. Drifting lazily, their nebulous forms were a stark contrast to the harsh landscape of red sands and salt below.

She heard a flicker in the sand beside her, then a light touch on her knee.

Two dark eyes regarded her curiously.

"Good morning," Kea whispered.

In reply, the meerkat gave a solid *phwap* of its little black tail against her leg, as if it was wielding a cane. The creature was so slight, she could barely feel the strike. Erect on hind legs, the meerkat was only twelve inches tall. Its forepaws dangled in front of it, as if clutching an invisible handbag.

"Are you a mirage?" Kea asked in awe. Arriving late last night, she yet to see the camp or its inhabitants in daylight.

The meerkat sniffed the air, twitching its tiny dark, wet nose. Its elegant black whiskers glistened in the sunlight. Coated in dark fur, its round ears stuck out from either side of its head, giving it the appearance of a monkey. The rest of the creature's fur was golden brown except for the exposed white belly.

The meerkat tensed, then scuttled up her shoulder to leap over the rim of her hat and land on top of her head. Another *phwap* indicated that the animal had settled into place.

I'm being used as a lighthouse.

They watched as the sun lifted ever higher above the horizon. Waves of amber raced across the great desert basin, setting alight the ochre sands. A smattering of trees and sage cast black shadows against the golden canvas. The sun's touch suffused her face with warmth, causing her to shudder in relief. The night had seemed endless, but she made it to see another day.

Breathe out.
Head over heart.
Heart over hips.

Using carefully measured breaths, Kea attempted to remain perfectly still.

Breath in.
Breath out.

"That's it," said a familiar voice behind her. "Don't think about Hazel sitting on top of your head."

Kea knew the scratchy syllables belonged to Professor Addison 'Addi' Rose, lead investigator of the expedition.

Hazel over hat.
Hat over head.
Head over heart.
Heart over hips.

"Or the numerous fleas and mites Hazel's carrying," he added.

Kea tutted. "We were having a moment," she said, shifting so Hazel could scamper safely down. She brushed her bangs out of her eyes and adjusted the brim of her hat. Her glasses had been knocked off kilter from a stray paw and she took a moment to bend the frame back into shape.

"I'm just trying to save you a few sleepless nights of scratching." Addi held out a leathery hand. "Come on. Tamaya's setting up some new cameras. She said she might need our help."

Kea wobbled to her feet, her legs unresponsive as blood sluggishly returned to her limbs. She held onto his hand until she could steady herself. "Sorry, getting old."

"You'll know you're old when everything hurts," Addi said, stroking his scraggly gray beard. He smiled naughtily. "And what doesn't hurt, doesn't work anymore."

Kea shook her head. Nearly six foot six, he towered over her diminutive five-foot frame. Although he was in his late sixties, Addi possessed an energy that never ceased to amaze her. On field trips, she and the students often struggled to keep up as he sprinted off to survey the next outcrop or channel section.

Addi looked toward the horizon, his eyes closed against the glare, like a cat soaking up a sunbeam. Before them stretched a vast white basin filled with a quivering sheen of blue. She knew the aquamarine was nothing more than a mirage, an echo of days long since past when the *vleis*, or pans, were filled with water. The ancient lakes had been fed by streams tricked into a dead-end relationship – the geographic depressions had no outlets. After a thousand years of baking under a cruel sun, their salt-rimmed graves were cracked, their undulating skins streaked by muck and mire from the recent rains.

Glancing down at her own skin, she saw that her pale arms were already blazing white in the morning sun. Realizing she had forgotten her sunscreen, she scooped up a handful of dirt and clay and smeared the particles onto her arms before lightly dusting her nose. Catching Addi's sidelong glance, she muttered, "If it's good enough for elephants, it's good enough for me."

Stray grains of sand trickled down her front, peppering her khaki pants. While much of her gear was rated for Icelandic conditions, she was relieved that some things, like her boots, field vest, and hat were universal. Underneath, her wrinkled t-shirt hugged her belly more tightly than she liked. The only plus of working in the Arctic was that winter fat could be hidden under layers of clothes. Out here, she was not going to be so lucky. Struggling into her field clothes had been a reminder that exercise, or dieting for that matter, were not a priority mid-semester. Thank goodness for elastic waistbands.

Addi waited patiently as she pulled on her rucksack with the blanket tucked inside the strap, his white panama hat unruffled by the breeze.

She cleared her throat to let him know she was ready. He flared his nostrils, as if taking one last sniff of the air. Then, with a satisfied grunt, he turned and headed back toward camp. Hazel scampered ahead of them, her little tail waving as she weaved through the yellow grass. The meerkat darted toward the perimeter of the meerkat colony, a dozen dark holes that gaped among hummocks of sand.

Tamaya was sprawled out on the ground near one of the colony entrances, her elbows knotted in a jumble of cables and plastic wrap. Spotting them, Tamaya waved excitedly, causing a length of wire to flail about and nearly thwack an undergraduate in the face.

Kea winced in sympathy. She picked up her pace, following in Addi's steps as he moved across the little hillocks of sand, treading lightly so as not to alarm the meerkats. Several of the animals kept watch above the entrances to the burrows, their furry heads swiveling back to track their approach. Deeming them acceptable, or at least not a threat, the animals returned their eyes to the horizon.

The clutch of students gathered around Tamaya treated their arrival in a similar fashion: glancing at them briefly before turning their attention back to the colony.

Kea sighed. Ever since she started sliding toward forty, she noticed that students of both genders ignored her. It was almost as if age had imbued her with the superpower of invisibility. While she didn't *want* their attention – indeed, she had found it incredibly awkward during her first years of teaching – their complete disregard for her was not an enjoyable sensation.

Crouching next to Tamaya, Addi gave his wife a little peck on her head, reminding Kea of another fact.

I'm single.

Again.

Tamaya sat back on her heels and grinned from beneath a charcoal-colored fringe. The rest of her hair was tied into a tight bun, its edges stained with ashen streaks and tinted with the crimson dust of the desert. Her nose, nothing more than a subtle pinch of skin, peaked out from between two bulbous brown cheeks. Her eyes had always captivated Kea, with irises as black as her pupils, their unexpectedly wide dimensions giving her gaze an unworldly aspect. However, the gap between her two front teeth and her inane goofy grin made her seem two decades younger than she really was.

Tamaya seemed unusually enthusiastic, which was always a bad sign. "Did you know that the locals call the meerkats 'sun angels,'" Tamaya babbled as she adjusted the tripod. "Because they thought that the meerkats could protect the village from the moon devils, which we would call werewolves."

Kea squinted. Numerous meerkats poked their heads in and out of their sandy holes, looking for all the world like a game of whack-a-mole. She found it difficult to imagine these wee critters fighting off a werewolf, even one suffering from lumbago. "Were these legendary meerkats armed with miniature AK-47's? Or perhaps little anti-tank grenades?"

"Do you know, I'm not sure?" Tamaya mused, as if taking the idea seriously. "I once saw an illustration with them wielding swords of some kind, but I can't remember where."

"No one asks the obvious question." Addi used his furled umbrella to settle onto a small rock. His knees popped loudly as he crouched.

"Why not lightsabers?" Kea offered. She saw Addi's eyes twinkle in response. She wondered if twinkling was a skill acquired over time, or simply the result of the degradation of the irises.

Addi shook his head.

Tamaya, who had probably heard her husband ask the question a million times before, replied quietly: "How big were the werewolves?"

"Exactly!" Addi raised the handle of his umbrella in exaltation and chuckled delightedly. "For all we know, these 'moon devils' could have been only three inches high!"

Tamaya waved at him with a spare hand, which Kea had come to learn was her friend's way of saying 'shush now.' She clipped a camera onto the tripod and casually tossed some of the plastic wrap away, intent on adjusting the lens. A breeze slapped the discarded plastic against her hair. If Tamaya noticed its clingy presence, she gave no sign.

Addi leaned over and gently peeled away the plastic wrap, and then, slowly and methodically, he started cleaning up the clutter of boxes and cables. Oblivious, Tamaya rammed wires into the device, connecting it to a miniature solar panel.

Kea noticed that the students sat close enough to observe what Tamaya was doing, but otherwise kept their distance, no doubt out of fear of pop quizzes. Judging by their sleepy expressions, she was not the only one who had a long night.

Rummaging in her pack, she unloaded various notebooks on the sand. Digging deeper, she discovered her sunglasses wedged beneath Zöe's house keys. *Guess I won't be needing these anymore...*

Kea traced the edge of the key with her thumb and felt the serrated edge cut into her skin. Her ex-girlfriend had probably changed the locks already.

"I found her beneath the baobab." Addi commented.

Kea shrugged. "Tamaya said it was the best place to see the pans...she was right."

"How'd you sleep?" Tamaya asked.

"Like a rock." Kea lied smoothly, making a note to raid the medical stores for something to knock herself out. She had already used up the supply her doctor had prescribed her. Although, as the last year had taught her, unconsciousness was no substitute for actual sleep.

Last night, however, her lack of sleep had little to do with her deteriorating mental and more to do with the couple shagging in the next cabin. Her private cabin, with its fluffed pillows, four poster bed, and sheets made of Egyptian cotton had looked gorgeous, but she had spent most of the evening staring up at the knot of the mosquito netting trying to block out the sounds of fornication. Finally, unable to bear it any longer, she went outside to seek solace in the silence of the desert night.

"Not staying up late working, were you?" Tamaya asked.

"Of course not," Kea replied automatically. "I made a promise. No geology. No drama. I'm here to help with your expedition, full stop." She surreptitiously tucked a battered copy of *Groundwater of the Kalahari* deeper into her rucksack. "This trip is all about you, I promise."

"What on earth is that?" Tamaya pointed at an object beside Kea's feet.

Kea scooped up the little plush toy that had tumbled out of her pack. "That's mine," she said. "Wherever I go, he goes."

Tamaya scrutinized the odd brown creature with blue feet and a flat blue nose. "Is that a platypus?"

Kea cocked her head. "Didn't everyone bring one?"

Seeing Tamaya's puzzled expression, Kea relented. "It was a present, from a friend." She averted her eyes. She had only told Tamaya an edited version of last year's traumatic episode on the Icelandic glacier, where two of her friends had been murdered. For some reason, providing her best friend with the gory details of how she had survived, seemed too daunting. *Or maybe, it's because I'm might not be the person you used to know.*

"That's Cletus." Addi pointed to a new arrival. "Genevieve's partner. Genevieve is the matriarch of the colony, but-"

"Cletus, although head male, is second string," Tamaya finished. "He'll do anything to keep in Genevieve's good graces."

"Good to be the queen." As Kea watched, Cletus began to preen Genevieve's fur. *No doubt excited to chow down on those fleas.*

She noticed that all the meerkats were wearing a thin sheen of black webbing. It resembled a backpack slung across their shoulders, fitted across the waist so it couldn't slip off. Cletus turned away from Genevieve, mounted a small rock, and struck a pose, as if modeling his sci-fi backpack for the paparazzi. It was quite fetching, she considered, if a little '90's. It would not have looked out of place in a back issue of *International Male.* "What are they wearing?"

"Activity trackers." Addi reached forward and scratched just under the edge of Cletus' pack. The little creature leaned into him, an expression of relief on his furry little face. "We designed them so they can groom each other, but tight enough so they don't slip off."

"Fitbits?" Kea marveled. "You gave them adorable looking fitbits?"

"We didn't design them to look adorable," Tamaya chided. One of the meerkats focused its deep, dark eyes at her and twitched its nose in a manner that made kittens look like hardened criminals. "They just have that effect on everything."

"The devices monitor heart rate, blood pressure, temperature, and location." Addi said proudly. "We can set baselines, even geographic boundaries, so if their heart rates spike, or one wanders outside the colony limits, we all get alerts on these." He patted the smartwatch on his wrist.

"We can even use the watches to tap into the cameras and see the live video feed. Smile by the way." Tamaya gestured to a lens mounted on a tall pole about fifteen feet away. "That's the public web cam. We have about twenty thousand viewers every day."

Reflexively, Kea looked around for somewhere to hide, to duck behind, anything to be out of sight of the camera, but there was nowhere to go. Forcing herself to take a deep breath, she turned sideways, blocking her backpack from the camera's view. "I always wanted to be an internet star." She said sarcastically as she discretely tucked the stuffed toy back into her bag. "Didn't you say this colony isn't part of the study, since they've been so habituated by the tourists?"

Tamaya nodded. "We use these guys to test out new gear. We have the whole colony wired for monitoring."

"Isn't that a bit expensive?"

"Our last documentary had over one million views," Tamaya said smugly. "We have loads of advertisers. Between the ads, coffee cups, mousepads, and toothbrushes, we're doing quite well."

"Meerkat toothbrushes?" Kea boggled.

"The people want what they want." Tamaya shrugged. "Who are we to question good dental hygiene?"

Kea, who had received crocheted meerkat wine koozies from Tamaya every Christmas for the last ten years, bit her lip.

Poofs of sand billowed into the air above the tunnel entrances, as if a dozen sand geysers were erupting simultaneously. "Morning cleaning," Tamaya said as she adjusted her wrist monitor. Kea noticed that as Tamaya moved her finger, the newly installed camera pivoted in response. "They're just getting their day started. And so should we." Tamaya waved 'up, up' to the students and Addi. "We'll all feel better after some coffee."

Addi led the way along the path, spinning his open umbrella against the crook of his shoulder as he drowned the gaggle of students with facts about the reproductive cycle of warthogs.

Walking along the path, Kea still couldn't quite believe that she was here. Only two days ago, she had been sleeping on the floor of her office in San Diego. Now, several flights later, and reeling with jetlag, she was standing knee deep in meerkats in the Kalahari.

She always envisioned the Kalahari to be full of endlessly shifting sand dunes and perhaps the odd spitting camel. During the flight, however, she had time to research the vast desert and learned that the landscape was more complex than she had imagined. Nearly six hundred miles across and spanning more than a thousand miles from north to south, the Kalahari contained a variety of realms. To the north lay the gentle, undulating sand sheets, composed of windblown red sand and remnants of sheet floods. To the west stretched the seemingly endless sand dunes, some more than two hundred feet high. Here, in central Botswana, lay the pans, dead basins of salt, the lands between marked by shrubs, grasses, and scattered acacia trees.

Holding a pack of tools and packaging under one arm, Kea fell in step beside Tamaya. It was her first moment alone with her friend since she had arrived late last night. "So," Kea began in a low voice, "are you going to tell me what's going on? Your voice mail

R.J. Corgan

was...troubling." She did not mention the series of phone calls or e-mails Tamaya had ignored except to confirm flight times and the logistics for arriving from Gaborone, the capital.

Tamaya half-shrugged. "Some cameras have gone missing. We're not sure what's going on, but we think it could be poachers."

"Poachers?" Kea was confused and more than a little irritated. She had dropped everything to come here, worried sick for her friend. "Meerkat poachers? Who on earth would even want...wait, is there even a market for meerkat pelts?"

Tamaya barked a strained laugh. "No...I mean, that's not what they're after. Everything has a price on its head out here, from lions to elephants. The rhinos around here are especially under threat." She paused at the perimeter of the resort and sighed sadly. "We just happen to be in the way."

Kea followed her gaze. Mackenzie Camp was a battered old big-game encampment that had been retrofitted a few years ago to take advantage of the eco-tourism industry. These days, Mack Camp, as it was known, was a five-star luxury resort, styled to exemplify a glorified version of nineteenth century expeditions.

Kea nearly wept at the sight of it. Elegant white tents, strung together like lanterns, rested on a dark wooden platform. The canvas walls that trimmed the main hall billowed like a massive cotton sail tethered to the wooden poles. She half-expected people to be walking around with pith helmets and offering to save the Queen. Instead, the current population consisted of undergraduates slouching around in khaki shorts, t-shirts, and baseball caps.

Behind the resort, Kea could see a collection of silver bubble tents, temporary structures erected for the undergraduates. She felt a pang of jealousy. Unlike her own meager Icelandic expedition that had been propped up by donations, a slender grant, and some bits of string, the advertisers sponsoring the numerous meerkat documentaries and the live web streams drew money in heaps that was funneled to expeditions across Africa. Additionally, Tamaya informed her, half of the profits went to help supply the local villages and schools. Beyond the student tents, Kea spied the lines of rectangular equipment tents, generators, aerials, and vehicles that receded into the distance. It was enough to equip a small militia.

Over the last five years, Tamaya had repeatedly invited Kea on the expedition, but Kea didn't accept. While Kea loved her friend dearly, having shared a dorm room in college, she was amazed the woman could dress herself, let alone keep fifty people alive in the middle of the African desert.

Addi was waiting patiently for them at the base of the steps to the main hall, but before they got within earshot, Kea grabbed Tamaya's arm. "What's really going on?" she pressed. "I didn't fly all the way out here to play *Die Hard* with ivory poachers. I'm a geologist, not John McClane."

"You're not here to be either," Tamaya said soothingly. "The park wardens assured us that they've got the situation under control. I just needed another adult around. We're a bit short-handed. Besides, that's only part of the reason why I asked you here. Tomorrow night Addi is..." she corrected herself. "I mean, *we* are going to make an announcement about the expedition, and I don't want to be alone. I'm so glad you came." She gave Kea's hand a squeeze. "You can't even know."

More worried than ever, Kea allowed herself to be led toward the main hall. The thrumming sound of insects around them seemed to cause the air to vibrate with energy, giving the impression that the camp was about to float off into the sky, taking her with it. "I'm not sure if this counts as fieldwork or a vacation," Kea muttered.

"We'll ask you that again in a few days." Addi chuckled as he climbed the platform steps.

"Shush," Tamaya reprimanded him, but made no move to follow her husband. Instead, she led Kea over to the nearby equipment cache and relieved her of the tools. "I've got to check if the batteries charged overnight properly. Why don't you grab some coffee and have an omelet or a scone, and I'll join you later?"

Kea paused, momentarily dumbfounded.

Omelets.

Scones.

Fieldwork my ass.

Before she could assemble an appropriate response, her eyes alighted on a large box sitting in a cart. The container appeared to be filled with the bodies of several dead meerkats, their eyes staring lifelessly up at the sky. "Are those...corpses?" Moving in closer, she saw that the creatures were three times the normal size of a meerkat, as if they were some genetic aberration concocted in the lab of a mad scientist. "They're gigantic."

"They're meerkat robots," Tamaya said patiently.

"I'm sorry." Kea blinked stupidly. "For a moment, I thought you said you said the words 'meerkat robots.'"

"They're not robots," said another voice. "They're closer in design and function to androids."

She turned to see Dr. Katherine LaFontaine – formerly Katherine Rose – standing behind them. Katherine was world renown for her work on mammals in the Kalahari, but more importantly, she also happened to be Addi's first wife.

Kea fumbled with the concept. "You mean they're...meer-droids?"

"Something like that." Katherine stepped between the other two women and heaved a spool of cable into the cart. She carried herself with such innate authority, Kea found herself mumbling apologies as she hastily stepped out of the way.

"We didn't build them," Katherine continued. "They're on loan from the Brits. The devices have built-in cameras so they can be placed within the colonies, and their fur is scented to help them blend in."

Considering them again, Kea saw that the meerdroids mimicked the creatures standing at attention on their hind legs. Lying in the cart, however, the pose gave them the appearance of rigor mortis. She tried to imagine them standing up in the pans, towering above their warm-blooded counterparts, King Kong meerkats of the Kalahari.

"I've only gotten one of them to work properly." Katherine nodded back toward the colony. "I've haven't even been able to get the batteries in the rest of them to charge." She opened a panel of one of the meerkat's posteriors and started pulling out components, cursing under her breath.

Tamaya leaned in to inspect the device, but Kea found herself zoning out as her nostrils caught a whiff of a familiar scent. *It couldn't be.* She sniffed again. There was no mistaking it. Drifting from flaps of the main hall was the smell of what could only be a waffle bar. Her stomach gurgled.

She turned back to find that Katherine was already walking away, a meerdroid in hand. "I forgot she'd be here." Kea never felt comfortable around Addi's ex-wife.

"She's the university's leading authority on rhinos." Tamaya shrugged. "She comes every season."

One of the dangers of dating within academic specialties, Kea thought, *was that there are so few jobs to go around.* Even in such a small circle, Kea felt outside of her comfort zone.

Poachers.

Robots.

Lions.

Ex-wives.

What could possibly go wrong?

"You okay?" Tamaya looked concerned.

"I'll feel better," Kea muttered, "when you tell me what's really going on."

Tamaya eyed Addi waiting at the top of the steps. "Remember to pack a lunch and we'll meet you by the jeeps in a half hour," she said loudly, as if for his benefit. Then, patting Kea's arm, she whispered, "We'll talk more later tonight, I promise. Everything's fine."

Kea shook her head as Tamaya walked toward the equipment tents and a knot of dread twisted deep in her gut. Tamaya was annoyingly talented at nearly everything at which Kea was abysmal, from differential equations to macramé, but like herself, Tamaya was also a terrible liar.

Chapter 2 – Safari Sock

THE JEEPS bumped and swayed as they trundled along the rim of the pan. Bouncing up and down in her seat, Kea was grateful she'd used the restroom prior to heading out to the field sites. Although 'driving' would be a generous term to describe the movement of the jeeps as they heaved their way through the shifting sands. Boating would be more apt, she reflected, as the jeep veered from side-to-side. The constant passage of the tires over the sandy track had resulted in washboarding, a by-product of physics that created transverse ripples, making the journey a chin-chattering ride.

"The colonies are about three or four miles apart." Tamaya called from the driver seat. She rested one hand lazily on the wheel as she nibbled on a scone, seemingly oblivious to the shaking.

Kea sat behind her, crammed in beside Dr. Gwen Floros, a geographer. While they'd only spoken at the annual interdepartmental meetings, Kea had no trouble remembering the woman. Cresting at just under five feet tall with hair styled like an exploding paint brush, she was hard to miss.

Gwen held a skein of wool in her lap, her hands deftly clicking away with her needles, creating what looked like a half-finished sock. The wool was dyed a deep blue and the garment was edged with elaborate stitching. The woman barely glanced out of the window, intent on her knitting, as Tamaya rattled off reams of meerkat facts. Since the students had been working the sites for over a week already, Kea assumed the lecture was for her benefit.

"The size of the colony depends on the number of meerkats," Tamaya continued. "It's all about having enough land to forage for food...oh my goodness!" She waved her arms in excitement. "Look! Springbok pronking!"

Kea peered out of the dirt streaked windows. Across the desert grasses, a dozen or so deer-like creatures grazed quietly, their heads crowned with curved black horns. Their fur was tan, save for a bright white belly and a thick brown stripe that ran down their backs.

"The springbok leap when they're happy." Gwen pointed at one of the creatures bounding across the grass. In a single leap, it jumped six feet into the air, appearing to soar effortlessly, covering thirty feet in a single jump. As the animal coasted above the grass, the hair on its back rose up, exposing a white, milky fur that rippled in the breeze. "It's called pronking."

Kea marveled as two more springboks leapt after the first. It was like watching Bambi try to fly.

Gwen elbowed Kea out of the way to get a better view. The woman held up the wad of kitting in front of her face and took a selfie with the animals in the background. Once she was finished grinning inanely at the camera, Gwen settled back into her seat. But only, Kea noted, after they'd passed last of the springbok herd. *No pictures for me, I guess.*

Seeing Kea's bemused expression, Gwen offered, "Sock loves pronking."

Kea could hear the capital 'S' when Gwen spoke. "That's...lovely," Kea said slowly.

"Sock loves all animals." Gwen lovingly smoothed the stitches in her lap. "I hope someday Sock will get to see a rhino."

Kea had taught Geology 101 for nearly a decade, so she knew that when a freshman was talking nonsense, it was best to humor them. At least until she could get out of a confined space, like this jeep. She nodded enthusiastically. "Has Sock seen a lot of animals?"

"On four continents," Gwen gushed. "And that's just in the last five years." She took another picture of the garment on her knee. "Very into safaris, is Sock."

"Five years!" Kea was baffled. "Isn't that rather a long time to spend knitting a sock?"

"It's not the *same* sock." Gwen sounded aggrieved. "It's more of a..." she trailed off as if searching for the right word.

"A reincarnation of Sock?" Kea offered. "Or a Sock gestalt?"

"Sock is a philosophy," Gwen replied severely. "Not a single entity."

Kea was saved from having to think of a response when the jeep made a sudden turn and veered down another track.

"This colony is led by a meerkat called Nikita," Tamaya practically shouted over the sounds of the jeep's engine. "The batteries on some of the trackers have gone a bit wonky, so we're going to see if we can sort those out and fix some of the cameras."

R.J. Corgan

Kea listened absently, her attention captivated by the knots of sprouting grass, the gnarled and twisting trees, and the rocky plains stretching out beneath an endless blue sky. Adrift in this new world, she wasn't certain how much time passed before the vehicle lurched to a stop. She tumbled out of the door and stood blinking in the sun, grateful to be on firm ground.

Addi's jeep swam up the track and juddered to rest beside them. The remaining jeeps, she presumed, continued to another colony.

"We'll have to walk the rest of the way," Addi said as he stuffed batteries into the backpacks of undergraduates who were lined up like pack mules. "This colony isn't habituated to our presence, unlike Genevieve's crew, so we've built a blind further in as a basecamp."

Once all the students were kitted up and watered, the team headed out. The students quickly fell into step behind Addi and Tamaya. Kea was content to take the rear, observing the team from a safe distance. She'd rarely met the faculty members on this expedition more than once before, and she was certain that none of the students had ever been in her classes. She was terrible with names, and faces for that matter, but she had an encyclopedic memory for annoying mannerisms. Scanning the students that plodded along the track in front of her, Hair-twirl Girl, Patchouli Dude, and Saggy Pants were all unknown quantities. She was hiking through the wilderness surrounded by complete strangers and the nearest hospital, or police station, was hours away.

The gnawing sensation in her gut returned.

I've been here before.

A year ago, she led a scientific expedition much like this one. When things started going wrong, paranoia consumed her, making her suspect everyone, often wrongly, until her friends began to die and she had to flee for her life. *Just swap sand for ice. Unless, of course, I'm just being paranoid.* She couldn't help but chuckle. *Oh self-doubt, how I didn't miss you...*

"Don't fall too far back," cautioned the man in front of her who had noticed her lagging. "You might get eaten by lions." In his late thirties, the man sported a goatee that would have made Errol Flynn proud. If he ditched the white t-shirt and cargo shorts for a green tunic and a pair of tights, he could get a job as Robin Hood. His name was Carter, Kea remembered, one of the adjunct faculty. Tamaya had

16

introduced him last night, adding, 'He's a botanist, but he only has a *master's* degree.' This statement had been pronounced with great sadness, as if the man carried a disease, although Tamaya's tone suggested that Carter's unfortunate condition could be treated with a light topical ointment. Or, perhaps, a Ph.D.

"You're kidding, right?" Kea shielded her eyes and scanned the brush and scrub for any sign of large predators. "Tell me you're kidding."

"Just stick to the path," Carter advised. "Snakes and scorpions are a bigger worry." He continued down the trail.

Kea swore under her breath.

"What's that?" Carter asked over his shoulder.

"All I had to worry about in Iceland was dodging puffin poo or dying of hypothermia." Kea searched the sands for anything venomous or slithery and quickened her pace to catch up. "You know, non-lion things."

She fell into step behind him and, despite her fear of being eaten, found her eyes drawn to the peculiar zigzag stitching of his shirt. Presumably once white, the cotton fabric had faded into a manila wash, perhaps bleached by a thousand days of desert sunlight, dust, and sweat.

Down girl.

"I got it in the rainforests of Papua, New Guinea." Carter replied when she inquired about its provenance. He paused as if remembering discovering it in some remote village bazaar. "Used to wash it by just holding it above my head in the rain."

For some reason, Kea found herself nodding, as if she too did her laundry in a rainforest on a remote Pacific island every Sunday.

"I was visiting the Asmat tribe," Carter continued. "Cannibals, of course. Or used to be. Lovely people, now. Well, some of them. They get a bad rap, you know." He pulled out the nozzle of his camel pack. "Back in the sixties, they made the mistake of eating a Rockefeller...Bit hard to come back from that, from a PR perspective."

Kea shuddered. "That sounds awful."

"I imagine it's all in the seasonings." Carter shrugged. "Not that they had time for any of that. They just speared him, cracked his head open, then tucked in. Or so the story goes." He stopped walking to take a long sip of water, then frowned.

She watched as he took his pack off, extracted a sachet of powder and poured the contents into the water bag. A fine cloud of dust drifted upward. Her nostrils caught a whiff of artificial cherry.

"It's all about power, you see." Carter shrugged his pack on again. "They believed that by devouring the flesh, you consume the power of the person you're eating-"

She cut him off with a wave of her hand. "Did that actually happen?"

"Well, the family never admitted it," he conceded. "It's agreed that he ran into a spot of bother with his boat and he swam to shore to get help. Twelve miles, if I recall. Likely have drowned, or so it was thought, until a member of the tribe later admitted to eating him. A week earlier there had been a bit of a kerfuffle with the Dutch, you see. They'd killed some members of their tribe, so when the tribe found him swimming to shore, well…revenge is a dirty beast."

Suspecting he was about to provide more details of the gruesome meal, she diverted the conversation by inquiring about the origins of his boots. He was still regaling her with tales of how he used them to cross the Sahara on foot in the company of a Peruvian folk band and a drag queen named Holly Galore, when they joined the rest of the team at the shelter.

The researchers had erected the blind beneath the shade of a large tree. Its vast, twisting canopy and stout trunk reminded Kea of a Dr. Seuss illustration. The shelter was thatch and wood, bolstered by rusty metal poles. It was large enough for them to hide their equipment from the colony but too small to properly shelter twenty or so students. The meerkats, for their part, seemed to be ignoring them anyway.

Once the laptop computers had booted up, their screens flickered with live feeds showing different views of the colony, including scenes from inside the tunnels. Scanning the landscape, Kea could see several cameras mounted on poles that marked the numerous colony entrances, but she was intrigued to know how they got the cameras inside the dens.

As Addi rattled off updates of the colony's inhabitants, Kea stood at the periphery of the group. The students had their notebooks out but weren't writing much down. Again, this lecture was presumably for her benefit, so she took out her own notebook and started duly scribbling some doodles.

Nikita was the dominant matriarch, while a male called Tripp was her mate. The professor named some other notable characters, including Samantha, the rebellious daughter, and Rascal, the adventurous, if unimaginatively-named, troublemaker. Today, it appeared that Samantha was staying behind with a couple of other meerkats to babysit the pups while the rest of the colony foraged for food.

Enjoying playing the part of tourist for once, Kea stepped away from the group to take pictures while Addi allocated specific duties to the team. While the colony was a good forty feet away, she could see a couple of meerkat sentries watching their team suspiciously as if they were shady shoplifters, harmless for now, but certain that at any moment the humans might do something sneaky.

The landscape, with its scrub, spikes of grasses, patches of soft sands, and brilliant blue sky, made every shot postcard worthy. Feeling the intense heat of the sun baking her shoulders through the fabric of her shirt, she stepped back into the shade just in time for Addi's daily 'motivational' speech.

Tamaya had warned her about this.

Kea settled down on crossed legs and pulled out a bit of scone. In Iceland, field breakfast consisted of instant coffee and a stale granola bar. The feast this morning had included quiche and cinnamon scones. "When I was a lad," she muttered quietly, "breakfast was a piece of cardboard that we'd eat in a ditch and we'd be grateful if we had mud to dip it in..."

"Can you sense it?" Addi asked the assembled students. He licked a finger, probed the air, then sucked his finger, smacking his lips, as if it had been dipped in marmalade. "*That* is the taste of the unknown. Every day, we see their morning rituals." He fixed each student in turn with a fierce glare. "They clean out their dens, they hunt, and they take care of their young, never knowing who will live to see the next sunrise."

Addi leant on his umbrella and clutched the bright blue handle with both hands. "A hundred different things could happen. An attack from a rival gang, a fatal bite of a snake, or death could swoop down from above at any moment." He lunged dramatically with his umbrella and smacked a baseball cap off the nearest student. The hat tumbled into the sky before Addi deftly snatched it out of the air.

"That is what we're here to study." Addi examined the cap curiously, as if it were an alien object. "How they deal with the unexpected. These creatures have an immensely complicated social hierarchy." He gestured flamboyantly with his umbrella, as if he were a wizard casting a spell with his staff. "Every day, different babysitters take care of the pups while the rest of the colony leaves to hunt. They alternate roles, but how do they decide who goes and who stays home? Who stands watch when they roam? It is this altruism that makes them so fascinating. That behavior benefits the group, so unselfish in its nature, yet it is a stark contrast to the ferocity with which the matriarch governs."

Kea picked apart the scone, intent on the bits with icing, as she waited for Addi to finish. She noticed that Tamaya was filming her husband with her phone, no doubt to upload to their web channel later.

"How did they evolve this way?" Addi asked the group. "What can we learn from them?" He handed the hat back to its owner and pointed an accusatory finger at the student. "What is it you want here? What is it you can help us discover?" He turned his head up to the sky and bellowed: "Why are we here?"

He lapsed into silence. The air was thick with expectation. The students shifted anxiously on their feet, eager to get started. Kea had always found Addi's theatrics at dinner parties exhausting and this was no exception. She could tell, however, that the students were hooked. If he asked for volunteers willing to spend the day weighing wildebeest feces, they'd probably all raise their hands in delight.

As the students dispersed into groups of twos and threes, Kea wandered over to Tamaya who was attempting to plug a cable into a laptop. "Is this before or after he's had his coffee?"

"He doesn't do coffee," Tamaya replied. "He says it addles his will." She slapped the laptop. "Come on, you tit, work." Despite her violent encouragement, one of the camera views remained obstinately dark.

"Can I help?" Kea offered. "I'm in a thump-something kind of mood."

<20>20</20>

Tamaya flicked through a dozen views on the monitor before switching back to the same dark screen. She swore. "Bad enough Boudicca's cams keep going down, now we're having issues here as well. It's like the network's cursed..."

While Tamaya tried to ping the camera via a command prompt, Kea's attention drifted to another view that displayed twenty or so meerkats running through the desert grasses. As they swept across the sands, they paused frequently to stand on their hind legs and spy for predators. Despite their size and ferret-like bodies, Kea was struck by the resemblance to monkeys.

"There they are!" Tamaya exclaimed as the screen finally came to life. "Pup cam is back online."

Despite herself, Kea let out a little 'oooooo' as five tiny pups emerged from the entrance of a burrow. Moving with tiny, awkward steps, each pup was more adorable than the last. They wobbled out of the hole and squinted in the sunlight under the watchful supervision of two babysitters.

"Only six weeks old," Tamaya narrated.

Barely bigger than her palm, the cubs tumbled and jumped onto each other as they wrestled. Occasionally the adults would intervene, but for the most part, the guardians seemed content to keep watch or groom each other.

Another meerkat approached the pups. According to Tamaya, this was Samantha, this colony's Jane Eyre. Samantha had something gray and translucent, dangling from her mouth.

"Here comes breakfast," Tamaya explained. "She's brought it back so they can learn to feed. Notice how she jumps about, tempting the pups to take the food from her mouth. She's bitten off the stinger until they're old enough to hunt them on their own."

"A meerkat romper room!" Kea cooed as she took pictures of the screen. "Do you ever get over the adorableness?"

"Samantha snuck out to another colony for a shag yesterday. When she got back, Nikita beat the crap out of her." Tamaya said wearily. "Nothing adorable about that."

"Teenagers are the worst, regardless of species." Kea concurred.

Tamaya swore again.

Glancing over, Kea saw that Tamaya had moved to another laptop, except on this one, none of the camera feeds were working.

"Must be a solar panel on the fritz again."

"Poachers?" Kea asked.

"It's possible, but then again it could just be a springbok used one of the arrays as a scratching post." Tamaya waved Addi over and showed him the screens. "We'll have to get it sorted. Take a group and see if any of the equipment has been damaged. I'll keep working on this end."

Addi dutifully knelt among the kitbags to extract the necessary tools, batteries, and cables. After pausing to dole out a few to each person, including Kea, he led the small group of faculty and students away from the blind, skirting around the perimeter of the colony.

As they walked, Kea was surprised by the amount of grasses, small bristly shrubs and flowers that bloomed like yellow stars in the brown sands and red rock formations. While the dirt floor was still cracked and parched from the sun, the sheer variety of vegetation was a stark contrast to what she had expected. She made the mistake of asking Addi about the plant life and was subjected to ten minutes of meteorological variables, the heartiness of succulents, and an extended lecture on the minutiae of photosynthesis, before he got around to mentioning the simple fact that the expedition happened to coincide with the rainy season.

Regretting ever opening her mouth, Kea had a moment of introspection. *Is this how students feel when they ask me a question about glaciers?* She shuddered.

They arrived at the first station, a metal pole five feet high, mounted with a camera and aerials. After a cursory examination, Addi declared that it was functioning perfectly and indicated that everyone should move on.

Kea noticed Addi waited to make sure that some students were watching, then he made an intricate sign in the air with his fingers that ended with a shoving motion of this palm, as if pressing the invisible symbol onto the camera.

"We're still doing the magic act I see?" she murmured as they continued walking.

Addi chuckled. "Which would you rather have for a professor? A grumpy old humbug, or one who might be a wizard?"

"Or just one crazy enough to think he's a wizard?" Gwen posited, not unkindly. Indeed, the woman had worn a subtle smile as she watched his antics.

"I know which I'd rather have." Addi's eyes twinkled. "Besides, life needs more mysteries."

"Speak for yourself." Kea muttered.

"Hush." Addi said suddenly, pointing with his umbrella.

Twenty feet away, a meerkat walked through the grasses, carrying something in its jaws. It dragged the object in the sand behind it, making chirruping sounds at another meerkat that lunged repeatedly at the prize, as if trying to knock the object away.

As they came closer, Kea saw that the meerkat was holding was an insect as long as her forearm and as thick as her wrist. As it flailed and thrashed in agony, she felt a shiver of disgust ripple up her spine.

"*Archispirostreptus gigas.*" Addi observed. "Giant millipede. It secretes a poison along its body to prevent it from being eaten. They're dragging it through the dirt to wipe the toxins off."

"That is revolting," Gwen said.

"They don't bite," Addi admonished. "Some people even keep them as pets." With a twirl of his umbrella, he continued walking.

Kea and Gwen watched in fascination as the meerkats continued wrestling over the still-crawling rear half of the creature, until one successfully gobbled a huge chunk. While it started to gnaw on its prize, the original hunter scuttled away with the rest of the twitching corpse, much to Kea's relief.

The next station was also operational, although Addi wanted to swap out the battery. While he worked, the others took a moment to rest. Kea used the opportunity to nip away behind some scrub and, after having inspected the area for anything lethal, had a pee. Returning, she found one of the men was regaling the group with what he evidently thought was a humorous anecdote.

Catching her, Gwen shook her head in warning, as if to say, '*don't make eye contact.*' Kea tried to beat a retreat to the bushes, but she was too late. The man had seen her.

Tristan was on loan from the data science department. Thin and angular, his posture seemed perpetually cocked just out of shape, like an abused paper clip. His long, hawk-like nose looked sharp enough to cut through steel, but from there down it seemed as if genetics had walked off the job. His Adam's apple was larger than his chin and his teeth seemed as if they had been stolen from a donkey. His skin was pale, spotted with the craters of acne scars. His eyes, partially hidden by thick glasses and an uneven sweep of dark bangs, widened in delight when he spotted her. He waved her over to join them, so she seated herself on a somewhat comfortable looking, and scorpion-free, rock.

"So, after the car accident," Tristan continued, "the woman said to the policeman, 'Officer, I don't know what happened. I swerved to the left, but the tree moved to the left...'"

Kea felt the pangs of a headache tickle the edges of her mind. Jet lag, she suspected, plus caffeine overload was starting to dull her senses. The heat probably wasn't helping either.

"'I swerved to the right,' the woman protested, 'but then the tree moved to the right...'" Tristan grinned inanely as he finished with, "'Madam,' the officer says to the woman, 'that was your air freshener.'"

Kea groaned. The man's jokes weren't just terrible, they were sexist to boot.

Gwen, who had been using the break to catch up on a bit of knitting, leaned in conspiratorially and whispered, "His therapist told him he was terrible with people. Advised him to learn a few ice breakers, so Tristan memorized a whole book of dad jokes and puns. We've been suffering ever since." She shifted on her rock, revealing a drawstring pouch filled with yarn that was attached to her belt loop with a D-ring. "The guy doesn't even have any kids. Or a wife, for that matter. Who would put up with that?"

Despite the ceaseless flashing of the knitting needles, Sock didn't seem to have grown much larger, Kea reflected. Or perhaps this was Sock 2.0.

"I try to get as much knitting done during the day before my Knightly Knitting sessions." Gwen pointed to a badge on her lapel that had two knitting needles entwined in the cables of a keyboard and mouse. "Even in the desert, I never miss an online session."

"I wish you would," Carter moaned from a rock beside her. "Every flipping night. Why can't you use headphones? I really don't want to hear a dozen people frogging at midnight."

"Frogging?" Kea asked blearily, her headache kicking into overdrive.

"It's the sound you make when you rip up your stitching." Gwen nodded with glee, holding her half-sock aloft. "Rip it, rip it." She mimicked tearing apart Sock, making what Kea could only assume was the sound of a frog being garroted.

Kea grunted. Whatever the couple in the next room next to her had been doing last night, it certainly wasn't drop stitch.

The team continued along the colony's perimeter until they reached the next camera station. The faculty were apparently taking advantage of this chance to reconnoiter, Kea noticed. Carter was collecting specimens of plants and meerkat droppings while Gwen used her table to record different species of birds, marking them on a digital map. Kea later learned that drones were usually sent to monitor the outlying areas or investigate damaged equipment and the researchers rarely got to walk the full perimeter.

Wondering why they weren't using a drone today, Kea reasoned that either Tamaya had sent the team out here because there's safety in numbers, or she had wanted to get rid of all of them for the morning so she could get some work done. *My money's on the latter.*

"Here's the culprit!" Tristan called, spotting the next camera. He dusted sand off the base of the pole and tinkered with a solar array that had been knocked askew. It appeared as if had been stepped on by something. *Maybe there is safety in numbers after all.*

Addi, satisfied that Tristan was on the case, wandered over to the shade of a nearby tree and was joined by the students. Kea remained with Tristan to help. She was light-years beyond exhaustion by this point and running on fumes. She reasoned that if she was going to suddenly pass out, at least she'd have the pole to hang on to.

"The power supply is now properly connected," Tristan mumbled as he traced the wires. "Looks like it was just a loose cable." He pulled out a tablet from his pack, shielding the screen with his hat as it powered up. While he waited, he sucked on his water bottle. She caught a whiff of watermelon and shuddered in revulsion.

Once Tristan confirmed the camera was running again, he showed Kea the display. The image of the colony looked different, as if embedded in a video game interface. "It's all part of the gamification." Tristan said, as if that explained everything.

"Gamification?"

"We get a lot of different types of animals passing through here. People get badges depending on how many animals they can identify. We crowd-source out ninety percent of the work."

"Handy," Kea conceded, although it seemed to take the 'field' out of fieldwork. "Outsource to whom?"

"Armchair Sarafians."

Kea blinked. "Are those in the Caribbean?"

"Tamaya calls them armchair ecologists, spread all over the world." He pulled up a screen capture of a wildebeest that had annotations calling out the different features of the creature. "We give cheat sheets for each species then the citizen scientists flip through the images on their phones and tablets from the comfort of their own home. As they identify the animals, they earn points."

"You trust people you've never met to mine your data holdings?"

"We spot-check a certain percentage for accuracy," Tristan added defensively. "Given the volume of imagery we have, their results are within an acceptable margin of error. We're not doing brain surgery, just tracking species. Right now, this is just phase one."

"What's phase two?"

"Machine learning. Eventually, the computers should be able to scan the live feeds automatically, as well as mine the historical feeds."

"Sounds very sci-fi," Kea commented.

"Around here, science is often fiction, or so it seems sometimes," Tristan said with a huff.

"What's that supposed to mean?"

"P-hacking," Tristan said with disgust. Seeing her blank face, he continued, "You know, in statistics where you look at all the data and uncover patterns that appear to be significant but aren't. Like associating the decrease in sales of licorice with the rise of socialism."

Kea noticed that he had lowered his voice. "Are you saying the research they're doing out here isn't statistically correct?"

"Rather depends on who you ask." For a long moment, Tristan seemed to deliberate, before shaking his head. "My job's just to keep the tech working. Come on, Addi's waiting."

Reaching the others sheltering beneath the shade of the tree, Kea was relieved to see that second breakfasts did not apply solely to her Icelandic field teams, or hobbits. Sitting on the cool sands, she devoured a cinnamon bun, then poured out a cup of lukewarm coffee from her thermos. Addi pointed out wildlife as they ate, but after he fired off the names of a dozen birds that she could not pronounce, let alone see, she found her attention drifting. She zoned out for a moment, then tuned back in when the conversation steered back to meerkats.

"The pups will soon be hunting," she heard Addi comment. "They should be feeding off scorpions with stingers soon."

"If meerkats are immune to scorpions, why take the stingers off?" Droopy Pants asked.

Addi tilted his head. "They're not immune. The adults can tolerate it, but not the pups. It would be lethal." He went on to explain that most people can be stung by a scorpion and be fine. "Unless you have a pre-existing condition, you're not going to die."

Kea's felt her terror of being surrounded by a desert full of miniature death machines recede. Slightly.

"Now, if you get stung by a puff adder," Addi continued, "that's a different story. Fortunately, we have a couple doses of anti-venom, just in case."

Kea did not feel reassured. "Is there anything else dangerous out here that I should know about?"

"All sorts." Addi said, gleefully. "Foxes, jackals, honey badgers, warthogs, and, of course, bogaratta pups, trechaworms, and helioscythes."

Kea was ninety-nine percent certain those last few weren't real, but Addi had already moved on to the next topic, the life cycle of the purple-glossed snake. He covered their digestive habits in such vivid detail that she didn't even notice that the others had packed up the remains of their food and were starting to move out.

Having completed a circumference of the colony and not finding any more damaged equipment, they headed back to the field station. They diverted briefly for a bit of frogging, in this case the kind with actual frogs. African bullfrogs. Carter's research, it turned out, was studying the amphibians that appeared alive and well in the desert, living in the muddy ponds that accumulated in the rains.

Kea didn't participate in any of the hunting and catching, content to leave that muddy adventure to Carter and the students. Fortunately, he seemed interested in keeping the specimens alive, and popped them into collapsible containers he carried in his pack. After collecting four frog specimens, they returned to the blind, pausing only for Sock to get his photograph taken with each caged frog.

Tamaya and her crew were tending to a sedated meerkat. While the meerkat's activity tracker was being repaired, the animal lay on his back in the basin of the weighing station, snoring quietly.

As Kea watched, Tamaya used a handheld scanner and read out the identification number contained within the rice-sized id chip embedded in the meerkat's skin. She read off more observations, which a student dutifully recorded, including the sex (male) and weight. Then, with a flick of a brush, she daubed a bit of paint just above the animal's hind leg to serve as an identifier. Within the span of a few minutes, the creature was ready to be roused and released back into the wild. Appearing a little groggy, he seemed in no hurry to get away, largely ignoring the group as they finished collating the data.

Kea noticed that Addi had sauntered off with a clutch of undergraduates, and was dancing around manically, apparently re-enacting a mother meerkat feeding her pups. The students lapped it up, even filming it on their phones.

She edged over to Tamaya and whispered in a low voice. "I have to admit, I used to wonder what you see in him." This was perhaps the closest Kea had ever come to addressing the twenty-five-year age gap that separated her best friend and her husband. "But out here, he's so animated. He's like a different person."

Tamaya grinned. "I first met him out on a safari. It was a different expedition, but he still had the same energy. It's like this place gives him life."

"And ulcers," Kea said, remembering Addi's latest health scare.

"That's just the undergraduates. They have that effect on me too." Tamaya said dismissively. She watched as her husband whirled and spun around the students. "It's this place, the sky, the sand, the animals…"

"…The constant threat of impending death," Kea added drily. "Did Addi mention the camera? It looked like it had been knocked over, possibly stepped on, which made me think of your poachers."

"Could be," Tamaya considered. "It could also have been an animal. I'll double check the feeds to see if they recorded anything."

28

"You don't sound very concerned."

"The poachers follow the game, generally, and there haven't been any game over here in the last couple of days. No one's willing to pay big bucks for springbok." Tamaya turned and looked at her in concern. "What's got you so down?"

"Sleep." Even as Kea uttered the word, she had to fight the urge to yawn. "Or lack thereof."

"Are you sure there isn't something else going on?" Tamaya pressed. "You haven't mentioned Zöe in ages. How are things between you two?"

Kea scooped a handful of memories out of her head and let them dribble onto the sand. A scattershot of images played through her mind: the glacier, pools of blood, the dead bodies of her friends, the flood that changed her life forever. While Tamaya knew broadly what had happened in Iceland, Kea had never provided details.

"Everything's fine," Kea reassured her. "I think I'm just having a hard time trying to figure something out." *Like, what I'm doing with my life?* "By the way, Addi was babbling nonsense just now. Treekaworms or something."

"You know what he's like," Tamaya shrugged. "He just makes up words if he can't think of any. Says it keeps the students on their toes."

"Really?" Kea frowned. "On the walk back, he seemed convinced that you've got an infestation of these worms in your garden."

"That wouldn't surprise me. Once we get home, I've been thinking of tossing the whole garden..." The monitor on Tamaya's wrist emitted the sound of a revving chainsaw.

Kea jumped. "What the hell is that?"

Tamaya examined the readout, concern etched across her face. "It's an alert. Looks like something's happened to Nikita's foraging team. Can't see anything on this tiny thing. Come on," she waved Kea over to the bank of laptops behind the blind.

"It's Rascal." Tamaya pointed to one of the many heartbeat monitors that filled the screen. "He doesn't look good." She tapped on another monitor and brought up a camera feed, tutting impatiently as she rewound the footage. "There it is. Oh, hell..."

Kea tried to see over the heads of the undergraduates who crowded in front of the screens.

"Cobra," she heard one of them breathe.

Tamaya's face was in her hands now. Kea had known her friend long enough to know that Tamaya was fighting to control her emotions, trying not to lose it in front of her students.

Nudging her way into the crowd, Kea used her body to shield Tamaya, to give her some privacy. On the monitor, a snake faced a line of meerkats. The creatures took turns lunging and striking, in an attempt to frighten the serpent away. One of the braver meerkats, Rascal, she presumed, led the charge. There was a sudden twitch, and then Rascal leapt backward, shuddering as the rest of the meerkats continued to harass the reptile.

On another viewscreen, she could see Rascal limping away from the group, his rear leg dragging uselessly on the sand. It was a pitiful sight.

"Didn't you say that adult meerkats could tolerate the venom?" Kea asked.

"They're remarkably resilient," Addi replied. "But they're not immune. They may survive the shock to the system, but the venom also has a necrotic component."

Tamaya breathed out a sigh. "It rots the tissue."

She's back. Thank goodness.

"Can't you do anything for the poor thing?" Gwen pleaded.

Kea had been watching the expressions of rest of the team. Now that Tamaya had recovered, the rest of the researchers and students appeared resolute. In contrast, the geographer seemed genuinely stricken by the wounded animal's plight.

"There's nothing we can do," Tamaya said calmly. "We observe, we record. If Rascal's lucky, he may heal. If not, let's hope it's quick…"

Judging from her tone, however, Kea didn't expect that a recovery was likely. She caught Addi watching his wife, his eyes filled with sorrow.

As the rest of the team split off to continue collecting data, Kea stayed behind to watch the injured meerkat on the screen, transfixed. Without the safety of the pack, without someone to watch out for predators, it was unlikely Rascal would even make it back, let alone survive the venom.

"I think," Kea whispered to herself, "I miss my glaciers."

Chapter 3 – Dinner and a Murder

AS THE researchers continued recording observations of the colony's inhabitants, the hours passed slowly as the temperature rose from sweltering to unbearable. Exhausted from several sleepless nights and suffering the almost hallucinogenic effects of jetlag, Kea felt like she could drop at any moment. When they finally returned to camp, Kea half-crawled out of the jeep, standing uncertainly. She wasn't sure she trusted her feet enough to get her back to the cabin, so instead, she lowered herself onto the steps in front of an equipment shed, watching as the rest of the teams rolled in. Scanning the horizon, she saw a solitary meerkat staring back at her.

The little head poked up above the grass, a good thirty feet away, its furry black ears backlit by the reds and yellows of the desert. The meerkat was a good distance away from Genevieve's colony, Kea noticed, not calling out or joining in the barks or chirps of the other meerkats. Aside from occasionally shifting its attention between the colony and Kea, it remained standing perfectly still. Waiting.

"That's Hazel." Tshepo's massive form caused the wooden steps to bow as he sat down beside her. Kea had been introduced to the camp's manager the night before and quickly learned that Tshepo knew as much about meerkats as the researchers, if not more. He had grown up around the camp, leaving only to attend school in Gaborone. His accent was gilded with Britain's Received Pronunciation and possessed a booming baritone that movie producers would pay big money to use in trailers. Regrettably, despite her many attempts, she had not yet been able to get him to utter the phrase, 'In a world...'

Tshepo pointed to the meerkat. "Hazel's a rover."

"A rover?" Kea struggled to remember the term from the many lectures but drew a blank. "Does that mean she's from a different colony?"

Tshepo shook his head. "She's been banished. Addi even took off her tracker."

"For what?" Kea frowned. "Did she accept an offer from the BBC without demanding a share of the merchandising?"

Tshepo looked at her, his dark eyes clear and focused, his brow low, his chin rigid. Kea had spent her life under the glare of fatherly disapproval, but Tshepo's ranked a nine: withering, with a whiff of sadness. He turned to contemplate the meerkat. "She snuck out for a shag with a male from a neighboring colony."

"Naughty." Kea found herself admiring the creature's rebellious streak. "Bun in the oven?"

"She had," he said sadly, "but probably not anymore."

"How so?"

"Genevieve found out she was pregnant and evicted her."

"Evicted as in..."

"Knocked the stuffing out of her." Tshepo took a drink from his bottle, wiping excess water off his chin with a swipe of his arm. "Then drove her out."

"Why?"

"The primary responsibility of being a matriarch is to keep her children safe. Genevieve already has pups that the colony is looking after. Hazel's children would be a drain of resources that Genevieve can't afford. Plus, Genevieve's pregnant again."

"Go Cletus," Kea cheered.

Tshepo made a sort of grunting noise, half in acknowledgement, half in annoyance. "Too many mouths to feed, not enough babysitters or hunters. Sometimes, if there is enough food and staff, the matriarch will let some of her daughters keep their babies. Other times, they evict them."

"Very nasty." Kea noticed Hazel looking longingly at the colony. "Hang on, if Hazel is Genevieve's daughter, Hazel's pregnant with Genevieve's grandchildren."

"Not anymore." Tshepo growled. "The stress of being evicted usually results in the babies being aborted."

"That's brutal."

"Could be worse, trust me," Tshepo muttered. "Besides, if Hazel bore the babies outside the safety of the colony, they wouldn't last long. Without the other members to babysit, to provide food, and with no warren for shelter..."

"But she's Genevieve's *daughter*!" Kea protested again. "She kicks out her own daughter, causes her to abort her own grandchildren, all for the sake of her own new kids..."

R.J. Corgan

Tshepo nodded.

Kea stared at Hazel, who was still looking pityingly at her siblings that guarded the colony from threats. Threats that now included her. "What's going to happen to Hazel? Can she join another colony?"

Tshepo pulled a face. "There's a possibility that Genevieve could relent and let her back in, but I doubt it. I suspect Hazel will stay away from the colony and just wait and see. All sorts of things could happen in a day out here. Who knows if even Genevieve will make it through the day as the leader?"

Kea knew he was referring to predators, but there was something else in his statement as well. Not a finality, exactly, but something bigger, something that had been nagging at Kea this whole trip. The pans, the Kalahari itself, were so vast, so big, it was as if Africa was elbowing bits of her brain aside to make room. The first time she had seen Iceland's fantastical landscape, she had felt a similar sensation overwhelm her, but this world seemed so much more dangerous. Vibrant, yet ruthless. "How long can she survive out there on her own?"

"She can feed herself," Tshepo admitted, "but she can't look out for predators at the same time. At night, she might find shelter from the cold in a hole somewhere, but, with no one to groom her, she's probably miserable from bug bites. To be honest, without her family to keep watch, predators have easy pickings of rovers like her."

"Can't she just join another colony?"

Tshepo shook his head. "Other dominant females won't want the competition unless their numbers have been severely depleted. Sometimes they start other colonies somewhere else. It's even possible she could fight Genevieve for control, but if she were a great fighter, she wouldn't be out there in the first place."

Kea watched the tiny figure, condemned and alone, so desperate to be let back into the family. All because of a quick roll in the sand. "That's awful."

"You get used to it," Tshepo said grimly. "Life is not easy here."

They sat together, watching as the last of the jeeps swayed up the trail. The vehicle unloaded its haul of students at the main hall before pulling up beside the equipment shed. As it came to a stop, a plume of dust rose into the air, painted ochre by the setting sun. Despite the patina of grit and clay on the windshield, Kea discerned two figures still in the vehicle, Katherine and Mani, the field equipment manager.

As part of her unspoken duty as Tamaya's best friend, Kea knew traditionally she was supposed to side with Tamaya on all things. However, fifteen years ago when Tamaya revealed that she'd been shacking up with her advisor, Addi, Kea had been torn. Still married to Katherine, the divorce had been sticky and according to Tamaya, had remained that way, as both Addi and Katherine worked in the same department. Tamaya, of course, had to be friends with everyone, even Addi's ex-wife.

Katherine was not by any means unattractive. Indeed, though she must be rounding sixty, she showed no signs of slowing down. Clad in the almost ubiquitous uniform of khakis and shirt emblazoned with the expedition's meerkat logo, her long, tanned arms were tightly muscled. She wore her long gray hair, the only sign of her true age, proudly, tied into a knot threaded with a red bandana. Attractive enough, Kea admitted, unless one was comparing her side-by-side with Tamaya, who had a two-decade advantage.

Kea made to rise, partially to greet them, but mostly to head for bed, but Tshepo held her back with a touch on her arm. She sat down in time to see Katherine throw open the driver side door, hurling insults into the cabin.

"All you had to do was maintain the jeep." Katherine yanked her pack out of the wheel well. "That's it, that was your one job. This thing nearly got us killed!"

"The jeep is fine. Or it would be, if you'd stop stripping the gears." Mani's voice was low and even.

Through the open door, Kea could barely hear his words, but she could feel the menace in it.

"This is the second time we've had problems!" Katherine sputtered.

"We had problems, because you put gasoline in the jeep this morning..."

"Exactly." Katherine flicked her bangs out of her face. "I'm the one doing everything around here!"

"The jeeps run on *diesel*. I had to drain the whole tank."

There was a long pause as Katherine processed the statement. Another moment passed before she noticed Kea and Tshepo watching from the steps. Katherine tensed, her fingers clenching into tight balls, her whole body shaking with rage. Then, as if a switch had been flicked, she turned on her heel and walked to the main hall.

Mani spat on the ground, closed the door, and drove the jeep toward the vehicle store, the tires ejecting another cloud of dust into the air.

Silence reigned once more.

Earlier in the day, Kea had watched the way Katherine handled the equipment, herded the students, and even how she bit into her croissant. The woman was deliberate with every motion, every stride, every word. Back at the university, Kea knew, students feared her. Even faculty members went out of their way to avoid going near her office door. There was no doubt in Kea's mind that should a pack of lions suddenly appear and try to devour everyone in sight, Katherine would be the last one standing, a flamethrower in her hand and a pile of dead lions at her feet. Considering Katherine was Addi's first wife, Kea shuddered to think what the divorce must have been like. Or how Addi had fared.

"Be surprised if she left him with even a spatula," she muttered.

"You say the strangest things." Tshepo seemed unphased by the dramatic events.

"All that," Kea waved her hands in the air at the departing vehicle. "Seemed a little out of proportion...even for her."

"Ms. Katherine had a shock recently." Tshepo's voice settled to a quiet hush, even though Katherine was out of sight. "A week ago, poachers killed three of the rhinos in her study."

"That's awful."

Tshepo nodded. "She had been observing them for five years."

Kea was not certain if he was implying that Katherine was emotional because she was upset her rhinos had been killed, or if their deaths had ruined her dataset. Knowing Katherine, it was probably both.

"Mani hasn't been helping the situation, however," Tshepo commented. "Although he has his own load to bear."

Something clicked in Kea's memory. Tamaya often talked of a particularly surly graduate student who had failed to pass his dissertation defense. Twice. After the most recent failure, the university had allowed him to stay on in his position as the department equipment manager, but with no degree.

The night before, Mani had picked Kea up from the bus stop at the nearest town, over an hour away. He hadn't spoken the entire ride. In his late twenties, the Pakistani's wide shoulders and full beard gave him the appearance of a much older man. His thighs were as thick as her waist, and his wrists as thick as her shin. His glasses, framed with faux Bakelite plastic, were worn and chipped, as were the lenses. Remembering his glowering eyes, she wondered how well he was taking their gratitude. *Still, a month for free in Africa, who would turn it down?*

Then again, she considered, after working for years under these professors and then having to fix their equipment, clean out their vehicles...

She rested her face in her hands. "Has it been like this all week?"

Tshepo rocked one massive hand back and forth, as if to say *sometimes yes, sometimes no.* "You take with you into the desert only what you bring." Then he lifted himself off the step and moseyed toward the equipment stores with long, slow strides.

It was a very Yoda-like thing to say, Kea thought, *and extremely unhelpful.*

Kea considered calling after him, to ask him what he meant, but she decided she was too tired to care. Bedtime was long overdue. As she stood, she noticed a figure in the distance standing beside Hazel.

After a moment, she recognized who it was and what it was doing and felt her faith in humanity was restored. Just a little. It was Addi, feeding the little abandoned meerkat a chunk of egg.

***

Afternoon tea, dinner, the coffee hour and cigars, all these luxuries Kea missed. She did not brush her teeth, she did not shower, she did not pass Go. She stumbled into her room, tossed her field bag into the closet, and collapsed fully dressed face-down onto her comforter. She closed her eyes and was instantly dead to the world.

It was glorious.

When she was finally roused by noises of the camp's morning preparations, she felt better than she had in a month. Or, if she were being honest, a year.

She gave the debilitating powers of jetlag a mental cheer for giving her a proper rest before enjoying a shower. It took her a full minute to realize that there was no shower head, but that instead the ceiling itself was the shower. When she managed to activate it, not only did water pour down from the ceiling in a perfect square of steaming rain, LEDs cycled in color from red to green to blue. Pressing another button caused the strength of the rain to oscillate, from a light mist to a downpour and back again. It took another minute to notice that the floor tiles were warmed from underneath.

From an environmental standpoint, she rejected the sheer waste involved. However, she found herself standing under the downpour for longer than she would have cared to admit.

After dressing and combing her hair into submission, she noticed that she had slept not only through the night but most of the rest of the day. *Some help I turned out to be.*

Cursing, she made quick work of brushing her teeth, astounded by the delicate porcelain basin and the gleaming hand soap pump, which consisted of a bright blue fluid encased in fluted glass. There was even a decorative meerkat resting atop the sink, which gave her a cheerful smile as she brushed. *Cute*, she thought, *but just a bit over the top.* Although, 'over the top' seemed to be the motto of this place.

It was only after she washed her hands with the blue fluid that turned out to be mouthwash, did she accept that she was just too low-brow for this place. The hand soap, Tamaya explained to her later, was in the meerkat: when the sensor at its base was activated, the neck compressed, dispensing a foamy soap out of its mouth. For now, Kea's hands were minty fresh, so she headed out the door, her thoughts bent on more important matters – food.

While the kitchens were preparing for late afternoon tea, she was able to wrangle some breakfast snacks left over from the morning's feast. She filled a plate with fruit, a yogurt, and a pecan braid and sat on the back steps of the main hall. Several of the student teams had already returned from a day in the field, but they kept to themselves, crowding around the tea trolleys. She was able to ignore the babble of their voices and focus on her pecan braid.

Priorities.

She had barely bitten into her pastry when a jeep raced up the road. She noticed that it didn't slow as it entered the camp's perimeter. In fact, it picked up speed, accelerating toward the medical tent.

Sensing something was wrong, Kea sprinted after it, her breakfast abandoned on the steps.

She wasn't fast enough. By the time she reached the tent, Carter had already whisked someone inside. Tristan remained outside, marshalling the students to make space around the doorway.

Kea jogged to a stop beside him. "What happened? Everyone okay?"

Tristan seemed irritated at being relegated to guard duty. "Addi's team was out in the field today and some of the kids tried to get a picture with some buffalo." He lowered his voice. "Morons. They nearly got impaled. Another one fell right off a small cliff. Katherine went mental."

"How's Addi?"

"Okay, I guess. Feeling guilty, probably." He pointed behind her. Kea turned to see another jeep had just dropped off Tamaya and Addi near their cabin. Addi appeared dazed as his wife led him up the steps to their room.

"And the kid who fell?"

"I'm no doctor, but looks like it was just a sprain," Carter said, emerging from the tent. "I've got his leg on ice. One of Tshepo's sons is going to take him into the village clinic for X-rays."

"Will he have to go home?" Kea asked. Having led field teams during times like this, she knew the logistics of extracting a student early could throw a whole expedition out of whack.

Tristan grinned. "As long as he can sit and use a computer, I've got data for him to clean."

"Lucky him." Carter caught Kea's eye and winked. "I'll see if he wants more pain killers."

***

Kea sat on a small rise, watching the sun hover low in the sky, as if it was not yet committed to its last sprint below the horizon.

Tamaya was still ensconced in her cabin with Addi, but Gwen had provided Kea with a list of chores that needed to be carried out. Kea, recognizing Tamaya's scrawled handwriting on the back of the envelope, had done the best she could. She ensured the spare equipment was cleaned and batteries were charged, checked the generators, and she even took a stab at indexing the travel receipts. Now she had nothing to do but wait for supper, and then, according to the list, help the students do all the washing up.

Gwen explained to her that each of the students gave one day of their time in the field to help sustain the camp. It wasn't that they couldn't afford local help, of course. The rotation was part of Addi's long tradition, based on his theory that it helped prevent the students from trashing the camp during their stay. Respect for a place, he repeated often, only comes from scrubbing its toilets. But these wise words were coming from a man who thought his combover was convincing.

Kea heard a familiar flutter in the sand beside her, followed by a hop on her knee, and then a slight weight as a meerkat mounted her shoulder. Hazel.

She followed the meerkat's gaze back to the colony. The other meerkats were returning from their hunt, scurrying across the field on all fours, their dark tails held high. The babysitters chirped in greeting. She watched as Genevieve and the others swarmed around the pups.

It was a warm and friendly sight, Kea thought. Unless you were Hazel. "Sorry kid," she told the trembling little creature. "You're welcome to crash at my place tonight."

"Don't feel too impressed, Hazel," a voice said from behind her. "She says that to everyone."

Addi walked up to her, rummaging in his pocket. He pulled out a plastic bag and took an egg from it. Crumbling the egg into small chunks, he gave bits to Hazel, who eagerly devoured them.

"I'm surprised to see you do that," Kea commented. She nodded at the bag of egg. "Doesn't that break all the rules?"

"This colony's not part of the study. The tourists have spoilt them rotten." Addi used a finger to scratch the meerkat's head. "Besides, it's not going to really make much of a difference for Hazel, except perhaps for tonight..." He gave her another morsel. "But of course, that's the old question."

"To get involved?" Kea ventured.

He rested his chin on the handle of his umbrella. "Scientific detachment is a powerful thing. If you can maintain it."

"I don't have much trouble with that in my line of work," Kea considered. "Although I mostly get paid to watch mud settle."

"I find myself faced with the question nearly every day." Addi sounded exhausted. "I see my favorite, Rascal, bitten by a cobra. Do I interfere? I have the anti-venom. What if Nikita gets bitten next? I could treat the wound, I could feed her children, but it would invalidate the study. Yet, that's one of the reasons I find being out in the field once a year to be so..."

"Horrifying?"

Addi shook his head. "Honest." His hands twitched frantically, as if he was attempting to pull the correct words out of the air. "*Momento mori*. This land reminds us of what it means to be truly alive."

He held another chunk of egg in his fingers, seeming to contemplate eating it before letting Hazel gobble it up. "If people saw so many, many things...But there's a filter, an intentional one, to shield them from the horrors of the world. You never meet your meat, never know your lunch. You're saved from having to make that choice, to see the consequences."

Kea had heard Addi give this talk before, but she had also seen him eat a baloney sandwich at lunch yesterday. She wondered why he was on this tirade now.

"Out here, there's no shielding, no protection. These creatures just survive. Or they don't." Addi tipped his hat down his brow, covering his gnarly eyebrows in shadow. "We all survive based on who we meet, who we encounter, how we communicate with them, and of course, on a bit of luck. Random, precious, luck."

Kea flashed back to that night in Iceland when she was laying against the crashed jeep, cold mud clinging to her clothes. She remembered wanting to give up, to surrender to the inevitable, of sagging against the tire as the iron jack slammed into the wheel well instead of her skull. She had been ready to die, yet instead, her decision to give up had been what had saved her. She softly repeated the phrase her therapist had ingrained into her, even if she didn't truly believe it. "Always chose life."

"Isn't that what they're doing, by accepting us?" Addi waved at Hazel and the colony. "Unlike most animals, they're very sociable with people. That should be an advantage. Yes, as a result more tourists feed them, but by that simple act of being kind with us, aren't they making a decision, one that could be an evolutionary advantage? One that could enable them to survive, by collaborating with another species?"

"Maybe," Kea considered. "But I don't think, aside from some pampered dogs and cats, that most animals would agree that teaming up with humans wound up being the best idea."

"It's something I think about a lot." Addi sighed. "Mostly because all of the tourists, all the students, everyone seems to want to coddle and cuddle these little beasts." He shook his head. "Listening to Tamaya, sometimes it feels like they're the children she's never had. Yet time and time again, we sit back and let them die."

Kea remembered Tamaya's expression when she saw Rascal limping from the snakebite. Tamaya was a scientist first and foremost, but Kea knew that she still cared. Bless her.

"I'd be lying if I said I didn't have any emotional investment in the colonies," Addi continued. "However, what we're trying to do is understand them to better secure their future, particularly those in captivity, so the best thing to do is to let them fight, breed, live, and die. Only through research, can we build a scientific base of knowledge to understand them, to learn from their social structure, and in so doing, maybe learn more about ourselves."

Kea noticed Hazel carefully following Addi's every moment, her nose twitching for another whiff of egg.

"Watching the colonies struggle, with predators, with starvation, knowing the right thing to do…" Addi seemed lost in thought. "As I said, it can be…troubling. Which is why sometimes," he said, handing more bits of egg to Hazel, "it's sometimes nice to not always do the right thing, but instead to do the *nice* thing."

Reeling from his barrage of words and suppositions, Kea found herself looking into his eyes and found them to be wet with wonder as he stroked Hazel's furry back. In that moment, Kea finally saw Addi for what he was: a young, wounded soul, trapped in the battered frame of an old man.

"Are you okay?" She had heard many different versions of the verbal beating Katherine had given Addi about the student's accident, all of them brutal. She felt conflicted. While the student's injury had been the result of his own actions, he had been under Addi's care at the time. Part of her wanted to ask Addi his side of the story, to find out what really happened.

Addi shrugged uncomfortably, as if sensing her curiosity. He shifted so he could sit by her to watch the sunset, or at least avoid her gaze.

Kea remembered falling into the ice that day back in Iceland, the sickening *crunch* sound as Tony's neck snapped under her weight, breaking her fall. Saving her life but ending his. The therapist had asked her again and again to explain what that felt like.

As Addi turned to walk back to his cabin, she saw that his cheeks were streaked with tears.

Kea knew exactly how he felt.

Hazel returned to perch on Kea's head. Together they watched as the fiery globe of the sun as it sizzled and flared, before finally sinking below the horizon. Clouds the texture of spun cotton stretched lazily across the sky, the spaces in between alight with blue and purple hues, before finally a burning a violent orange.

When it was time for dinner, Kea gently lowered Hazel to the ground, noting that the meerkat's gaze never wavered from the colony. It was heart wrenching.

"I'll be back with snacks," she promised, although she knew she could only keep Hazel alive as long as the expedition remained, which would be less than a week. It was just postponing the inevitable.

"Isn't that all I do anymore?" she asked the stars above as she walked back to her tent.

It doesn't matter anymore. Nothing matters. It's almost over.

Kea trembled, trying to shake the voice out of her head. The dark mantra had slipped into her head ever since she had broken up with Zöe. Ever since then her life started to unravel, and her sleep had become invaded by nightmares.

I know that depression lies, but in this moment, it feels like it's speaking a terrible truth.

***

Stepping into the main hall was like walking back in time. Tall mahogany posts were placed every twenty feet, the space between filled with sheets of white cotton that billowed whenever the wind gusted. Lanterns, elegant affairs adorned with black metalwork and gleaming glass panels, dotted the posts and rafters. No doubt intended to house extravagant wedding receptions, the tables were draped with reams of cream cotton cloth that stretched the length of the tables, with students crammed the benches on either side. The hall echoed with the incoherent babble of undergraduates.

Desert Hogwarts.

Tamaya ushered Kea to a seat at the faculty table and called for wine. At the other end, she saw Addi smiling and nodding politely as if nothing had ever happened. Kea watched in disbelief as someone pulled out crystal goblets rimmed with gold.

Tristan caught her eye, a goofy grin on his face. *Oh no.*

"Mahatma Gandhi walked barefoot most of his life," Tristan stated with glee, "giving his feet a tremendous set of calluses."

Tamaya poured a glass of wine for her before she retreated to the safety of Addi's side. Tshepo and Carter sat at the far end, leaving Kea with only Katherine, Gwen, and Mani as conversational companions. *Thank God for wine.*

"Mahatma also ate very little, which made him rather frail." Tristan's voice dribbled down the length of the table. "With his odd diet, also he suffered from bad breath."

Kea downed her first glass and poured herself another, noting and ignoring Katherine's frown of disapproval.

"This made him..." Tristan drew out an extended pause, obnoxious in its duration. "A super calloused fragile mystic hexed by halitosis."

Kea groaned. No amount of wine was going to make this evening better. To evade another onslaught, she tried eavesdropping on the conversation next to her.

"You must know by now," Katherine said to Carter, "there are many aspects to the life of the meerkat, which are challenging. It is a society dominated by females..."

"That's hardly unique," Carter replied.

"Of course not," Katherine sounded offended. "I was simply going to point out that the social complexities of the colony arise due to the competitive nature of the females. Even so, the murder rate is quite striking."

Mani and Gwen muttered in agreement, but Kea felt as if she had missed something. She held up a hand, feeling like a freshman at her first college lecture. "I'm sorry, the rate of what?"

"Murder," Katherine replied matter-of-factly.

Kea felt the hairs on the back of her neck stand up.

Tamaya nodded. "Meerkats have the highest murder rate of any species. Including humans."

"Out here?" Kea scoffed. "From who? The meerkat, in the lobby, with the knife?"

"The females have a nasty habit of killing other pups," Katherine expounded, fiddling with her phone. "It's a competitive thing, an assertion of dominance. The lead female may kill the young of the subservient females. With no children of their own to take care of, the females are able to provide more time to the matriarch's offspring." She held up her phone, showing an image of a meerkat's bloodied mouth leering up from the torn throats of meerkat pups. "A mother will do anything to ensure the survival of their children."

"That's horrible." Kea shuddered. *And why is that photograph the wallpaper on your phone?*

"It's not to say that subservient females don't also try to kill the dominant female's young," Addi offered. "Murder, it so happens, is part of what keeps the species strong. It's all in my book. Hasn't Tamaya given you a copy?"

Kea deflected the question. "Are you saying that murder makes them stronger?" It was difficult to reconcile what Addi was saying, given this was the man who just an hour earlier had been feeding Hazel bits of egg.

"It's a question of resources and ensuring the survival of the young," Katherine added. "After all, we're all just one breath away from poverty or death, either through an illness, natural disaster, or you name it. Jealousy, anger, all those emotions are there to protect our progeny. Meerkats are just more honest in their actions, although that doesn't mean they're not devious how they go about it."

"In my experience, I haven't found anything positive about murder." Kea said quietly, "Only...waste."

Much to Kea's relief, food came to the rescue in the form of bowls filled with what looked like a meaty stew over polenta.

"*Seswaa*," Katherine said in response to Kea's questioning look. "Goat meat. It's traditional."

After some careful sniffing, Kea tried a taste. It was surprisingly palatable, particularly with chunks of onion and salt.

The staff, she noticed, were two thin women who moved with bowed heads and only the occasional flash of a smile. These were Tshepo's daughters, or so Tamaya told her. They slipped in and out of the kitchen, placing the food on the table in silence. The students had to make do with a buffet. *Poor things.*

As Gwen rattled off new knitting stitches that she was learning, Kea slouched in her chair, using Katherine as a protective shield to avoid engaging in the conversation. Watching from across the table, Carter appeared to be attempting to smirk, but it was hard to tell. It was as if his facial muscles were fighting back.

Kea was relieved when Tamaya called for the table's attention by tapping a knife against her glass, saving them from Gwen's lecture on the merits of the Estonian brioche-stitch.

"We are sad to inform you that, after many years, this will be the last field season." Tamaya placed a hand on her husband's arm. "Addi will be retiring this year and I wouldn't want to continue the work without him."

Given the amount of money and technology lavished on the expedition so far, Kea wondered how the university felt about the decision. The problem with research expeditions led solely by academic institutions was that once the people running them left or retired, the research tended to stop. Any new faculty joining the university tended to pursue their own interests. It made studies of observing long-term processes particularly difficult.

"But we do have more than enough data for many more years' worth of publications," Addi chimed in. "And we can continue to remotely monitor the site from San Diego. Tshepo has offered to help maintain the equipment and we'll still send out a small team to tweak the instruments annually. However, this will be our last mass expedition with the students."

"We'd like to say thank to all of for being a part of this great experiment," Tamaya continued, extending many gracious thanks to each of the researchers.

Kea found her attention drifting until her eyes settled on Addi. He looked deflated somehow, as if Tamaya had just pulled the plug on him. *What would it be like if someone took my Iceland project away from me?* Kea wondered. *It's all I have left...*

Once the meal was cleared away, Tristan continued honking at his own attempts at jokes, while the rest of the diners made their best attempts to ignore him. It was apparent, however, that everyone was stunned by the announcement, no doubt consumed internally about what they were going to do for research without the expedition. Mani was the first to make his leave from the table and stomped outside.

Kea tried to speak with Tamaya but found herself pinned down by Gwen who queried her on the 'scientific' topic of the benefits of vortexes at a health spa in Arizona. Before she could break free, she noticed that Addi had left with Carter to check on the equipment stores.

While failing at terminating the conversation with Gwen, Kea was able to eavesdrop on Katherine and Tamaya's conversation. She couldn't make out much, as they were speaking in hushed tones, but she was certain she heard the words *'restraining order'* and *'Gwen'* in the same sentence.

"I wish..." Kea blurted out. *Too much wine.*

"Wish what?" Gwen asked, oblivious.

"I said," she looked around for another topic, but settled for faux honesty. "I could use a good segue right about now..."

"Oh, I hate those things," Gwen tittered. "I'm always terrified of falling off."

An awkward pause followed until Tristan leapt in. "That reminds me of that time I farted in an Apple store and everyone got mad at me." Tristan did not even wait for a response before finishing with, "It's not my fault they didn't have Windows."

Seemingly outflanked, Kea reached across the table and opened another bottle of wine.

***

After supper, even with help from the students, washing the dishes seemed to take forever. The staff had vanished already, content to let them finish up. When they finally dried the last plate, Kea found herself staring at the bloated and wrinkled skin on her hands, wondering if she had any fingerprints left.

Once she was certain that the kitchen was properly shut down, she headed back along the porch that lined the outside of the main hall. She paused at the edge of the platform to stare out into the blackness.

The light of the hall hid the stars above and draped the desert in a cloak of darkness. The temperature drop was equally startling. A world that had baked and sweltered under the African sun only a few hours ago was now chilled by the frigid blackness of the night.

Hazel was out there somewhere, she thought sadly. Probably holed up and shivering, alone. *If she was lucky.*

Kea shook her head. In her time working on the outwash plains and glaciers of Iceland, she had often felt small and insignificant, but she had never experienced this sensation of pervasive dread. Of being alone. Of being Prey. *Well, once.*

She firmly shut down that train of thought and made her way back to her cabin. *Not tonight,* she thought. *Tonight, we sleep. Tomorrow...well, I'll work that out tomorrow.*

Walking through the camp, she could hear the *thumpa-thumpa* of music coming from the students' tents. There was a clunk followed by the sound of a bonnet slamming near the equipment stores, probably Mani messing around with the jeeps. She made her way down the little alley between the cabins. *More like luxury huts,* she thought. They were decked out in the same quasi-colonial style as the grand hall, complete with porches, white cotton curtains, and lounge chairs.

Tamaya and Addi still had their lights on, although the curtains were drawn. Katherine and Tristan's cabins were dark, indicating they were either asleep or elsewhere. The lights were on in the next two cabins, although she wasn't sure which was Gwen's, and which was Carter's. The lights of one snapped off as she approached, and she thought she saw the twitch of a curtain. She quickened her pace lest she be caught staring.

Crossing the last few feet to her cabin, she secured the flap and drew the curtains. Her room, compared to her standard two-person tent should have seemed enormous, however in the span of two short days she had somehow already managed to clutter much of the floor with clothes, both clean and dirty, unstable piles of books and papers for grading, and clumps of her discarded field gear.

The bed had been made, so it seemed the staff had been in to tidy; however, they had obviously shied away from touching any of her belongings. Except her platypus. Her stuffed toy lay nestled in the pillows, gazing at her with its tiny black eyes.

"At some point," she told it, "when we get back, we're going to have to work out what we're going to do about being homeless..." She glanced at her watch. "One week from now."

Platy stared back uselessly.

"But not tonight," Kea assured it, her mind heavy with other thoughts.

She was certain that Tamaya's announcement was the reason Kea was here. However, after dinner her friend had dodged any attempts at conversation. She wouldn't even make eye contact. Which was beyond bizarre as this announcement was clearly why Tamaya asked her to fly out here. *But why? Just for moral support? Or was she worried that someone might respond poorly to the news that the expedition was shutting down?*

Everyone had certainly appeared surprised, but she had sensed disappointment in their expressions, not retribution. Everyone, that is, except Katherine. She was the only one who seemed unperturbed by the news. Mani did appear angry, however, 'disgruntled' appeared to be his default setting.

Kea lay back on her bed, eyes closed, and counted out long breaths to calm her mind. When that didn't work, she popped a few sleeping pills. The arms of Morpheus, however, remained elusive.

Instead, she flipped through some work emails. It was the usual demands from students for better grades, notifications of mandatory trainings that she was behind in, and reminders that she was late on submitting slides to a conference. There were some other administrative emails about security issues in the office, but she glossed over them. In desperation pulled up a paper describing new statistical techniques being applied to modelling groundwater flow regimes in Alabama but after twenty minutes of reading, she never once felt like nodding off, which was disturbing. It was a bit like drinking a liter of vodka and not feeling the slightest bit inebriated.

She picked up the desk clock and glared at it accusingly. It was almost one in the morning, yet she felt more awake now than when she had first crawled into bed.

R.J. Corgan

When the screaming started, it was almost a relief.
Almost.

Chapter 4 – Spied Her Man

THE TERRIFIED wail echoed throughout the camp like a thunderclap. Thwacking away the mosquito net, Kea staggered out of bed, her arms and legs entangled in its clingy embrace. Breaking free, she fumbled for her glasses, yanked on a pair of sweats and sandals, and dashed outside.

The campground was alight, the air filled with panicked voices as manic shadow puppets danced against the fabric walls of the student tents. One by one, the luxury cabins illuminated as the faculty woke. The darkness between the cabins was filled with flickering shadows as a dozen brave, flashlight-wielding students ventured into the darkness, searching for the source of the scream.

As Kea ran, she spied the gray flicker of scorpions on the path ahead, skittering away in alarm. She paused, considering going back for proper footwear.

The scream came again.

Tortured.

Feral.

And it was coming from Addi and Tamaya's cabin.

Kea bolted down the path, praying her pounding feet would scare away any of the vicious creatures, because there was no way she was going to let them get between her and Tamaya.

"Get back!" she yelled as she crashed against a wave of curious undergraduates who had beat her to the cabin. Gaping and whispering at the entrance, they pressed against the door, blocking her way. She used her slight form to her advantage, ducking and weaving through their mass, before she managed to enter the room.

Inside, Addi writhed in agony on the floor, his pajamas half-twisted off. Mani and Carter knelt beside him, attempting to administer first aid. Tamaya, dressed in only a t-shirt and shorts, was caught half-in and half-out of bed, peering dully through the torn wreckage of the mosquito net at her husband. Her eyes were wide, Kea noted, as if not comprehending the sight unfolding before her. *Shock. Not good.*

51

Mani cradled Addi's head while Carter pulled off his own shirt and tied it around the old man's left leg. Even from where she was standing, Kea could see that Addi's foot was swollen, the big toe red and angry, the size of a plum. The slipper on his right foot was still on, the other lost somewhere among the jumble of clothes and gear scattered across the floor.

"Tshepo!" Carter called.

"Here!" Kea heard the man call from outside the doorway.

"Bring the jeep round." Carter turned his attention away from his patient to bellow at the doorway. "We need to get Addi to town, now!" He seemed to notice Kea for the first time. Their eyes locked. The intensity of his gaze finally snapped her out of her own stupor.

"Med kit!" they said simultaneously.

Kea turned, hesitating. "Snake? Scorpion?"

"Not sure yet. Get anything you can." Carter's voice was calm, yet urgent. He checked Addi's vitals methodically as he talked. "We'll need bandages and tourniquets too."

"On it." Kea elbowed her way through the crowd. Gwen was on the patio, ushering the undergrads away, clearing a path.

Nodding her thanks, Kea pelted down the stairs and dashed across to the equipment store. The hut was unlocked, thank goodness. She slammed the light on with the palm of her hand and scanned the interior. Wireframe shelves stretched down the length of the room, filled with linen and other supplies for the guests. The expedition's field gear hunkered in a far corner, its dirty canvas bags and the black shells of the survey equipment seemed foreign in this room filled with fluffy towels and dry baked goods.

The large white emergency kit was kept on a rack by the door. The shelf next to it contained other medical supplies, including cough syrup and sleeping pills, all neatly stacked. Lifting the kit off its supports, she tossed the box on an empty shelf. She grabbed a plastic bag and tossed in extra gauze, IV packets, tubes, bandages, painkillers, anything she else could find. The extra anti-venom supplies, due to their expense, were kept in a locked box in a cabinet. Carter would have the key.

Rather than wait to unlock it, she used a can of beans to smash the glass, grabbed the box, and tucked it under her arm. Then, pausing to retrieve the large medical kit, she bolted out the door.

52

Once she stepped outside, she was blinded by a pair of headlights as a jeep screeched to a halt in front of her. She heard the door of the vehicle thrown open and, before she could react, Mani snatched the gear out of her hands. She followed him to the rear of the vehicle as he tossed everything into the back of the jeep.

As her eyes adjusted to the light, she saw Addi on the floor of the vehicle, wrapped in blankets and pillows. Tamaya was beside him, holding his hands, her eyes filled with tears. Tshepo was at the wheel, Carter beside him, barking into the radio. Mani slammed the door shut and slapped the rear of the jeep with his hand, twice. There was an eruption of dirt and pebbles as the tires tore into the sandy track and then there was nothing except the dim glow as the taillights receded into the desert night.

"I'll get on the sat phone and call the hospital, and let the university know," Mani said before running back to the vehicle store.

"Addi was probably just up for a pee," Gwen said in a quiet voice.

"Always check your shoes," Katherine added primly. "Scorpions get everywhere."

Kea turned to see Katherine clutching her arms against the chill. The woman wore a white night gown that probably cost more than all of Kea's wardrobe combined. Gwen was dressed more sensibly in flannel pajamas and an obnoxiously long knitted scarf trailing from her neck to her feet.

"That seemed like a bit of an extreme reaction for a scorpion sting…" Kea muttered.

"Snake?" Katherine posited. "Cobra or adder? More likely an adder, I'd think."

Kea felt her heart slowing down as the adrenaline created by the drama receded like a tide. She forced herself to breathe deeply and jammed her hands under her armpits to keep them warm and to hide her trembling fingers.

Beneath the glamorous night gown, Kea noticed that Katherine was wearing bunny slippers. Incongruous as they were, the woman still managed to look amazing in the silly things. Kea wondered how well they would hold up against fangs.

Kea shuddered. "I'm not sure what it was that bit him, but we'd better find out. The doctors will need to know in order to treat the bite properly."

Gwen groaned. "The students…"

Kea had the same thought. God forbid the kids started poking around the room on their own. The last thing the university needed was a dead student. *Again.*

They jogged all the way back to Addi's cabin, Kea and Katherine letting Gwen, in her sensible sneakers, lead the way along the sandy path. As they approached the cabin, they saw a smattering of students lounging on the porch smoking cigarettes. Ignoring their ranks, Kea forewent the steps and leapt lightly onto the elevated wooden patio. To her relief, she saw no students inside the room itself. Now that the excitement had died down, she assumed the others had either gone back to bed or wandered back to the main hall for a late-night snack. *No doubt on their phones, sharing the night's adventure with the world.*

While Gwen checked the patio, Katherine probed the darkness beneath the bed with Addi's umbrella, which left Kea with the closet – and the slippers. *I'm really starting to hate these women.*

Against her better judgement, she approached Addi's abandoned shoe on all fours. Holding the slipper at arm's length, she gently shook it.

Nothing happened.

No vicious critter fell out. Nothing slithered or hissed.

Relieved, she dropped the slipper near the rumpled pile of Addi's jacket and suffered a minor heart attack as a creature scuttled out from beneath one of the sleeves.

Kea scrambled backward and fell against a table lamp. She howled an undignified yelp as her fight or flight instincts mentally slammed down on the **FLIGHT** button.

Things I hate, screamed her mind as she abandoned all reason, kicking and flailing in terror. *Things I hate, this thing I hate!*

Primal fear kept her kicking and thrashing, moving backward until she felt the solid frame of the bed press against her back. She paused, allowing her mind to take stock, to look for an exit, to size up her opponent.

The creature was the size was of her hand, with eight long and furry legs. Its dull brown carapace consisted of two globes that were tightly welded together at the middle, while its rear was large and studded.

The spider was running straight at her. Far, far too quickly.

"Get away, get away from me!" She pulled herself up onto the bed. Her thrashing hands found a pillow. In a blind rage, she threw it at the spider.

It missed the creature by a good foot.

"We have to capture it!" Gwen reminded her. "To help treat Addi."

As if responding to her voice, the spider made a beeline for the door.

Kea's arm brushed against a plastic cup, knocking it off the bedside table. She dove after it, her fingers slipping on the beads of water that clung to its sides. She cantered after the spider on all fours, the hardwood clocking against her knees that clicked and creaked in protest.

The spider raced across the threshold and across the patio before leaping down into the darkness of the sands below.

Scooching after it, Kea let out a horrified yelp as her momentum carried her over the edge of the porch. She landed in an undignified heap, face-down on the cold desert sand. The only thing that prevented her from screaming bloody murder was the thought of the spider, or any of the scorpions she may have just belly flopped onto, leaping into her open mouth.

There were flashes of light behind her as the students flipped on their camera-phones. Not, she suspected, to be of any actual help, but more likely to ensure that her faceplant, and buttocks, were preserved for all posterity in high-resolution detail.

In the pools of their camera lights, she was surprised to see a meerkat standing in the darkness not ten feet in front of her, its forepaws clutched to its chest.

Hazel, Kea guessed.

In the splay of shadows that lay between her and the meerkat, Kea saw a flicker of movement.

"Don't move!" While she was addressing the spider, the students obediently held their lights still. Either that or they were enlarging her buttocks.

The flicker happened again.

It was then that Kea realized she was staring at the *absence* of the spider. There were legs poking out of the sand, but no body. There was another shiver of sand and two of the eight legs vanished. *It's burying itself.*

"Oh no you don't!" She whacked down the cup where she had last seen it. "Paper, paper, paper." She ordered. She wished she could calm down, wished this thing did not freak her out so much. It was only the memory of Addi writhing in agony that kept her focused on capturing this creature while her instincts shouted at her to *get away, get away, get away!*

Someone handed her a drink coaster. *Of course it was a coaster, all good fieldwork required coasters.* She slipped it into the sand as deep as she dared before lifting the cup, sand, spider, and all.

"Gotcha!"

Agitated, the creature glared back, tapping its legs against the clear plastic. Staring at the furry appendages in revulsion, she struggled to resist the urge to drop the cup.

"You lot," she ordered her paparazzi. "Get close. Take pictures. Hell, take video. We need to get this to Carter, to the doctors at the hospital." She carefully reverse-crawled back up onto the platform, shuddering at the thought of what she might be crawling over. She placed the cup down on the floor and let the camera crew get to work.

Glancing back, she noticed Hazel was gone, hidden by the dark of night.

"Phone number?" A student asked.

"Here." Kea practically yanked the phone out of the student's hand and tapped in Tamaya's number.

Assuming Tamaya took her phone with her.

Kea remembered seeing friend huddled under a blanket in the back of the jeep, wearing nothing more than a t-shirt and shorts. Clearly still in shock. No phone, she realized, just as the voicemail kicked in. *Crap.*

Kea didn't know anyone else's number. "Gwen, get the phone roster, go, go, go!" After the little woman tumbled off down the ramp toward her cabin, Kea knelt on the floor and pressed her face close to the ground to examine the creature. "Now then, what the hell are you?"

The elongated front legs possessed small pincers. Those claws, combined with the flat front of the spider's head, resembled the profile of a crab. Her knowledge of spiders covered only daddy long legs and tarantulas. She had been quite content to keep her distance from spiders her entire life, until now. "There's never an arachnologist around when you need one."

She paused, realizing that someone on this expedition probably *was*.

The ***click*** of a phone next to her ear caused her to jump. Looking over, she saw a student drop the image of the spider into a search engine. Within three seconds, it returned a result. The student expanded a web page so Kea could read the text.

"Six-eyed sand spider. *Sicarius hahni.*" Kea read out, her tongue tumbling around the Latin. She expanded the description. "Oh, holy hell."

"What is it?" The student tried to peer over her shoulder at the screen.

"Deadliest spider in the world," Kea read out. "Of course, it is…" She scrolled down a little further and more information and photographs of the spider appeared. One sentence stood out, and not quite knowing why, she covered it with her thumb. "Mind if I keep this for a bit?" Without waiting for an answer, she headed across the camp to her own cabin, nearly bouncing off Gwen as the woman returned, a scrap of paper in her hands.

"Got the numbers." Gwen panted.

"Thanks," Kea said, taking the list. "I'll let everyone know." She pointed to the spider. "Can you find somewhere safe to keep that?"

Gwen frowned at the trapped creature but nodded and began to shoo away the students.

Reaching her cabin, Kea shoved a lump of laundry off her desk and booted up her laptop. Squinting at the list of numbers scribbled on the paper, she dialed Carter's number. "How's he doing?"

"Not great," Carter replied. "He's stopped screaming…Although I'm not certain that's a good sign."

"Listen," Kea set her phone to speaker mode. "I think we caught the thing that bit him. It's called a sand spider." She took a picture of the student's phone with her own. "I'm sending you a picture of it now. It's not good news I'm afraid."

"Is there an anti-venom?"

"Ummm…" Kea hadn't thought to look. *Getting old.* "One sec." She skimmed the entry, reading out the text as she did so. "A sand spider can go for a year without eating, doesn't spin a web…basically it just sits in the sand and waits for something to pass, and then it pounces."

"Anti-venom?" Carter prompted impatiently.

"Yeah, yeah. Let's see," she kept reading. "Here we go. The spider's venom has two toxins. One is necrotic, which means it destroys tissue and cells, but more dangerous than that is the second toxin, that's hemolytic. Looks like it essentially destroys red blood cells, which can cause hemorrhaging or worse."

Silence filled the digital space between them.

"It sounds horrible," Carter said eventually.

"Nothing here about an anti-venom," she continued, "but there may be a very good reason for that." She glanced over to make sure no one followed her to her cabin. Her eyes returned to the sentence she had withheld from the student. "It's probably because are no actual confirmed cases of anyone being bitten by one."

"None?"

"Two suspected, but not confirmed. However, in both potential instances the victims died. Fairly painfully. It says the spiders are actually very non-aggressive," she paused, remembering how she found Addi. "To be fair, if it was in his slipper…Addi probably scared the hell out of it. When I found it, all it did was try to run away, after the initial confusion that is."

"What are the odds of it being in his shoe in the first place?"

"I have no idea," Kea admitted. "Judging by the name, it lives in the sand…" *Which is everywhere.*

Carter grunted a "Thanks," then hung up.

"You're welcome," Kea said to dead air.

She tossed the phone onto to the desk, then fell backward onto the bed. The adrenaline was now little more than a trickle. Having found the spider and relayed the information, all she could reasonably do now was wait and get some rest. She exhaled a deep breath and contemplated another long night of staring at the mosquito net, drowning in her own night terrors.

Mysterious death.

Middle of nowhere.

Surrounded by strangers.

This wasn't her first rodeo.

I should have t-shirts printed...

She used her laptop to send a group e-mail to let all the faculty, including Gwen and Katherine, know she had reached Carter, then, somewhat reluctantly, forced herself to get up off the bed. She put on some decent clothes and sensible footwear before heading back out into the cold.

There was no way she was just going to lie around wondering what was going on.

Not again.

***

The lights were on inside the tech tent which was odd, considering it was two in the morning. Poking her head through the flaps, Kea found Tristan hunched over a laptop. Black and white images danced across the screen. Around him, the folding tables were littered with stacks of papers, extension cords, and abandoned coffee mugs. Equipment of different shapes and sizes were plugged into various hard drives and laptops.

She rustled the flap a bit more to announce her presence. Tristan turned and waved her inside. Kea forced a smile. The man was between her and her goal: footage from the camp's cameras that might have recorded anyone going in or out of Addi's cabin. *Am I too late? Did he already delete the data?*

She moved across to a canvas chair, removed its current occupant, a wad of discarded potato chip wrapper, and sat down. "What are you doing up?" She hoped she sounded convincingly casual.

"Couldn't sleep after...all that," Tristan waved in the general direction of Addi's cabin. "I'm trying to do something productive and keep working on building the neural network..."

Seeming to interpret her expression of frustration as one of curiosity, he continued, "A neural network is an artificial version of the human brain, made of nodes that make decisions." He pointed to the image of wildebeests displayed on the monitor. "In this case, we're using it to analyze imagery." He must have noticed her glassy eyed look, as he paused and started again. "When you came into the tent just now, you walked past some field equipment stacked on a couple of folding tables."

"Okay," Kea said slowly.

"What did they look like? How high? What color?"

"Ummmm…" She was desperately trying to think of ways to get rid of this guy but for the life of her, she couldn't remember any details of what the tables looked like.

"Our brain doesn't need to spend a lot of time looking at every table we pass to know it's a table," Tristan continued. "It just notes the general 'table-form' and moves on. If we spent every minute of every day micro-examining everything that we looked at, we'd never get anywhere." He waved at his laptop. "Using the same technique, a computer can be trained to rapidly identify basic forms, and then examine the form at even higher levels of detail. But to do that, the computer first needs an inventory of training images, like the mental database that's already in your head."

"Fascinating," Kea grumbled. All she really wanted was for him to bugger off, so she could get a look at the campground's network of cameras. Not that she was familiar with their systems or software…she supposed she could ask him for help. While she had no reason not to trust him, everything about his body language, his honking laugh, his Everest-sized nose, and those awful jokes, irritated the crap out of her and made her naturally suspicious.

"Of course, real life is never that simple," Tristan blathered on, oblivious. "It's easy to teach a computer what an aerial view of a plane on a runway looks like, but it's a different story when you have a hand-held image taken on the ground of a plane, with the sky, some fences or trees, or a person's head in the way on the image, for example. Your brain figures out that it's a plane because of all the planes you have seen in your life and you're filling in the gaps that aren't on the image. Computers aren't that clever yet. Well, some of them are. *We're* not there yet." Lecture completed, Tristan turned his back on her and typed merrily away on his keyboard.

It was clear that he wasn't going anywhere, possibly for hours. Frustrated, she grappled for relevance, or perhaps a way to get something useful out of the man. "What does this have to do with meerkats?"

Judging by the look of delight on his face, she'd evidently made a mistake. He seemed much more animated now. "While we can get the computer to identify the general form of a meerkat on an image," he prattled, "it's much harder to get it to identify the markings we paint on their fur. Anytime the software identifies a meerkat with a known pattern, within a single frame, we're able to document that. It's very helpful to identify individuals, particularly when they go missing."

"Missing?" Kea frowned. "Don't you track all of them with fitbits? How can you lose them?"

"Only our colonies have the trackers. If we can get the machines to identify individuals by their gait and mannerisms, we wouldn't even need the marks. This will be used at a much larger scale and would be much less intrusive. We already have hundreds of thousands of hours of video from this site alone."

"Where do these missing meerkats go?"

"Sometimes a predator gets them. Sometimes they're actually driven out by the dominant female or killed during skirmishes with other meerkats."

"Grim," Kea said, her mind returning to Hazel. She frowned at a screen displaying an enlarged image of a pattern painted on fur. She watched Tristan label the image with the meerkat's name and a six-digit number. "What happens to the rest?"

"Hmm?"

"When the computer can't identify them. What happens to all of those images?"

"Ah," Tristan tapped a pile of tablets. "That's when our crowd sourcers come in, remember? They identify frames we can't do automatically. Not just the meerkats, but anything caught on camera."

Kea, remembering his earlier lecture on the armchair ecologists and perked up. She lifted one of the tablets. "May I?"

"Of course," Tristan replied. "You can also download the app on your phone. The app will give you some of the images, but not the full catalog of course. They're loaded with the last couple of day's data, so we can at least do a quick skim in case there's something important, or something we missed."

"Can I keep this?"

"Sure." He waved his hand at the pile of devices. "We've been farming the work out to undergrads to keep them busy in their downtime, so another pair of eyes will be good."

He's being nice, she thought. *Damnit.* She always found it harder to despise someone when they were being helpful. She considered the sprawl of unfamiliar electronics and computers on the desk that were no doubt password-protected. "Look, I was wondering," she began, resigned. "I wanted to see if any of the cameras that have a view of the campground..."

He jabbed a finger into the air. "...did they record anyone going in and out of Addi's tent?"

"Well, yes," she said, somewhat deflated.

"Already checked." Tristan stated as if it was the most obvious thing in the world.

"You can have a look for yourself." He opened an e-mail, put her name in the "To: line," typed in a directory path, and pressed '*Send.*' "The link should get you to the folder in the cloud with the video files. They're sorted by time and date. I've already made back-up copies, in case there's something I missed, or if the authorities want a look."

Perfectly sensible. Alarmingly efficient. It made her despise him even more.

"What made you even think to look?" she asked. "He was bitten by a spider in his bedroom, not beaten with a candlestick in the library."

Tristan nudged his glasses up to the summit of his nose. "Dunno. Just felt like I should check, I guess. Addi has a lot of friends, but...sometimes the old bastard's kind of an ass."

Kea had seen Addi take on some of the deans at the university and was forced to admit she agreed with his assessment. "Aren't we all sometimes?" She held up the tablet. "Thanks for this."

His nose was already pressed against the screen of his laptop. He barely acknowledged her departure. "Knock yourself out."

***

Kea stared at the two little pills on her bedside table. Encased in transparent bubbles of plastic, they sat hunched on their silver foil base, as if patiently waiting to be set free. She had liberated the pills from the remaining medical supplies on the way back to her tent, using the pretext of cleaning up the mess she had made in the medical stores earlier.

A flash of Addi's face, contorted in pain, filled her mind's eye.

With a decisive shove, she tossed the pills into a drawer and instead focused her attention on the tablet. *No time for sleep.*

She had already watched the night's camera footage. The devices were primarily pointing at the meerkat colonies and any coverage of the campground was incidental, but she was surprised how much she could see. However, aside from the general dispersal after dinner, evening trips to the bathrooms, and the odd batch of undergraduates lighting up, the footage was unremarkable.

One camera had an unrestricted view of Tamaya and Addi's lodge. She saw both enter the tent shortly after dinner. Aside from two trips to the bathroom, no one else went in or out all night.

The resolution wasn't good enough to see anything as small as a spider crawling inside the cabin, of course. The webpage said that six-eyed sand spiders could survive for more than a year without a meal or a drop of water, so there was no telling how long the creature had been inside.

She reviewed all the files for the last week but saw no one going in or out of the room other than Addi or Tamaya. The cameras only showed the front of the cabins, however. Windows or other entries were not covered. *A real 'locked room' mystery*, Kea mulled. *But when the walls are made of linen, does it matter? Is there such a thing as a locked-tent mystery? If there was even a mystery at all. This being the Kalahari, the spider could simply have just wandered in.*

At that thought, Kea got down on all fours and ensured that her tent was spider free. The canvas walls were not made of cotton, she saw, but some artificial material, likely waterproof. The shower had walls to support the utilities, and the bathroom door had a lock on it, thank goodness.

She crawled back into bed, tucking the netting in tightly around the mattress. She kept her slippers up on the bed as well, not trusting herself to remember to shake them out in the morning.

After two hours of pouring over all the footages, she was no more the wiser than when she started. There was nothing to see.

Nothing at all.

That niggled at the back of her head. She felt like she was seeing shadows. In Iceland, her suspicions had proved right, even if she had gotten everything else terribly wrong. *I am right this time?*

She pulled up the learning app on the tablet Tristan gave her and stared at the training images to see if they contained anything useful. Dozens of little meerkats flashed across the screen, with prompts at the bottom asking her to fill in their names. One after the other, she noticed the images either didn't fully capture the markings painted on the fur necessary to identify the animal, or even worse, the images were nothing more than blurs. The images were rejects, ones the computer could not process.

"I need more data," she told the funnel of the mosquito netting above her head. Unfortunately, she knew that, having exhausted the digital world, getting more data meant talking to people in the real world. *Before more people start having 'accidents.'*

Unless, of course, she was just being paranoid. That loop went around and around in her head until the blackness finally consumed her.

Chapter 5 – Urinalotta Trouble

ENTERING THE main hall, the scents of hazelnut, cinnamon, and bacon greeted Kea's nose like long lost friends. The bready smell of muffins heralded all the carbohydrates that would find their way into her tummy. The anticipation gave her hope that she might manage to make it through another day. After only two hours of unconsciousness – she could not accurately describe it as sleep – she was amazed she was even vertical.

Approaching the coffee station, she noticed that the crowds of students split before her, as if she were Moses parting the Red Sea. Well, her mood was foul, she reasoned, no doubt her breath was as well.

A glance at her phone that morning had shown no calls, no texts, and no e-mails. If there had been word on Addi, Tamaya hadn't tried to contact her.

She filled her cup and then, just to be safe, poured herself a second mug as well. Pausing to savor the coffee's aroma, she found herself staring at her reflection in the silver urn. *Oh hell.* Her hair was spiked out in all directions, resembling a thicket tangled in dental floss. Her sleep wrinkles were perfectly preserved on her face and although her reflection was distorted by the cylindrical urn, she was certain she could see a crust of dried drool plastered on her chin.

No wonder the students had given her space. She looked very much like a used bandage someone had left wadded up on the floor of a public toilet.

She closed her eyes and let out a long breath.

Her colleague might be dead. Her best friend might be a widow. She needed to have the strength to help them. She could shower later. Right now. Coffee and waffles.

Lots of waffles.

Trying not to spill any of the precious black fluid, she wandered over to an empty table, giving off what she hoped was her best '*stay the hell away*' vibe. She made two trips to the waffle station and loaded a plate devoted solely to crepes.

R.J. Corgan

She returned to find Gwen sitting at her table taking pictures of Sock, artfully arranged between plates of croissants.

Of course.

Kea wanted to bark something to scare her off, but concern overrode her morning grumpiness. "Any word on Addi?"

Gwen bit into a muffin and shook her head, scattering crumbs about as she did so. "No one's heard anything yet."

Kea counted off lumps of sugar from the dish. "Well, that might be good." She plopped four of the cubes into her coffee. "I think."

"Is it?"

"Schrodinger's cat," Kea sipped. Luke-warm. *Ugggh.* "As long as we don't know he's not okay, he's still okay."

Gwen tilted her head. "Or dead."

"We won't know 'til we know," Kea repeated firmly in case any of the students happened to be listening.

Putting down the muffin wrapper, Gwen dumped Sock on the table and started to knit. "What do you think the rest of the expedition will be like?"

"What do you mean?" Kea counted off four more lumps and put them into the second cup.

"With Tamaya and Addi gone…"

Kea sensed something akin to glee in Gwen's tone. "What do you mean?" she snapped. "They're coming back." *Unless you know something that I don't…*

The *Knightly Knitting* website archive had revealed that Gwen attended the virtual the knitting group the night before – Kea had checked. The woman had even lectured a group of German ladies on the importance of square knitting needles during mealtimes. Helpful fact: they will not roll off the table during a dinner. *I've learned far too much about knitting.*

Despite the alibi, Kea struggled to remember the comments she had overheard the night before between Tamaya and Katherine about Gwen. Something about a restraining order?

"Of course, they're coming back," Gwen said soothingly. "I just meant, what are we going to do with the students? If we let them sit around all day, they're bound to get into trouble. You know what they're like. They've already probably started tarting up meerkats in little outfits and posting photos of them on Instagram."

Images of meerkats in sailor suits and tutus flashed across Kea's eyes. Adorable, possibly. Exploitive, definitely. Not, she agreed, the purpose of this expedition. "I'll ask Katherine and Mani – wait, don't you usually take the student teams out to the field sites as well?"

"I'm a geographer, not a biologist," Gwen tutted. "Although I did take a few biology classes in undergrad with Tamaya. I'm strictly hands-off on these expeditions. I help with the mapping, but I leave all the leading to those two."

No doubt 'those two' referred to Tamaya and Addi. Kea mentally chewed over different ways to ask the question, but finally decided that she did not care if she offended the little woman. "I heard someone mention something about you and a restraining order."

"That old thing." Gwen brushed away the comment with an expression of mild distaste, as if she had just walked into a cobweb.

"It's real, then?" Kea asked.

"Yes and no," Gwen replied, returning her attention to her knitting. "I mean yes, it's real in the strictly *legal* sense of the word."

Kea struggled to think of any other option. "How in the 'not real' sense?"

Resting her needles, Gwen appeared to become fascinated with the remains of her muffin wrapper. "Since we must work in the same building and, like this, on the same expeditions, the restraining order only applies off-campus."

"Of course." Kea pretended to understand. While Kea worked on the city campus of Burlingame University in downtown San Diego, Gwen and the others worked out of the newer Lakeside campus, where Kea rarely ventured.

"It only applies as neighbors." Gwen sighed. "At home."

"Where things are not so good?"

"Not good as such, no. Although," Gwen looked around to see if anyone was listening. "I really do claim to be on the side of sanity on this one. Which is not a side I'm commonly on, or at least I certainly don't feel that way around this crowd. I mean, I can only spend so much of my life talking about urinals."

Kea's concern for Addi's well-being, and her own lack of sleep, was putting her dangerously close to losing her temper with this woman. "Is this conversation going to make sense anytime soon?"

"His urinals," Gwen repeated, as if it explained everything.

"Look, I'm sorry. I really am trying to follow-"

"She didn't tell you, did she?" Gwen shook her head in disgust. "They own the property between our houses. It's essentially a vacant lot, but Addi wants to build a commercial building for his start-up company."

"Okay, not getting the urinal angle," Kea pressed. *A start-up?* Tamaya had not mentioned anything about any of this, which was troubling. Was this Addi's plan to stay flush in retirement? *So to speak.*

"Yeah, well, that's what a sane person would think," Gwen agreed. "Due to existing zoning codes, the town wouldn't let him develop the property. Residential only. Even though two houses down there's a gas station."

Kea tried to remember the neighborhood where Tamaya and Addi lived. They usually met up for drinks after lunch or brunch on the weekends, so it had been years since she had been to their house.

"Addi clearly thinks he's in the right," Gwen continued. "So, as an act of protest, he's filled his empty lot with toilets."

"Toilets." Kea repeated dully.

"I'm not making this up." Gwen pulled out her phone and started flipping through photos.

"Is that allowed?"

"Again, the question of a sane person." Gwen nodded sagely. "He claims that they're part of an art installation. He's planted plastic flowers in each toilet. See?"

Gwen showed her a picture of a row of commodes, their porcelain skin glowing a dazzling white under the bright sunlight. The toilets stood proudly on the grass field, their bowls overflowing with soil and bursting with fake flowers. Then another. Then another.

"How many?" Kea gaped.

"At last count, eighty-seven."

The toilets were disturbing, Kea admitted. Oddly artistic, but still not something one would expect from a college professor. She paused, reflecting on the varied personalities of some of her co-workers. Maybe a field full of toilets were exactly what one would expect from a dotty old professor. Still, what bothered Kea the most about the photographs was that Tamaya had not mentioned these little beauties. Not even in jest. "And the urinals?"

Gwen flipped to another photo. "He mounted those on trees. Painted them bright red, with dancing Kokopelli figures. Not sure who he got to paint those...they're quite good, so I doubt he did them." Her finger lingered on an image of a urinal emblazoned with a Batman logo. "I quite like that one."

Kea still felt as if she was missing something. Several somethings. A busload of somethings. "How does a restraining order come into play again?"

"Ah," Gwen grumbled, "That would be where I came into play. With a sledge hammer. Against said urinals."

"Because..."

"He's destroying my property values," Gwen protested. "He's a lunatic."

Said the kettle of the pot. Err...Potty. Kea shook her head. "And this smashing occurred in daylight? In front of witnesses?"

"Well, no," Gwen admitted. "I did it at night. Thought I could blame it on drunken college students. But the bastard had a camera mounted in a tree..."

Kea could not help but laugh.

"Which I knew about," Gwen sounded hurt. "I took it out first."

"Of course, you did."

"It was the second camera under the eaves I didn't know about." Gwen lifted another muffin and ripped off the top. She pinched off bits and squished them into little balls that she popped into her mouth one at a time. "The restraining order only applied to property. Well, his property." She chewed thoughtfully. "I think, in theory, the judge was on my side, but there's nothing anyone could do legally. Not until...I mean well maybe now...that he's...if he's...not okay."

Kea found that Gwen was looking at her in a peculiar manner. The woman reached across the table and grabbed Kea's hand. Kea tried not to flinch at the touch.

"I hope he's okay, I really do," Gwen pleaded. "I mean, he's a pain in the ass, but..." Her gaze flickered away again, as if remembering the scene last night. "I wouldn't want *that* to happen to anyone."

Not too long ago, Kea would have left it there, but she was no longer that person. Not anymore. "You must admit," she pressed, "from a certain point of view, you'd be relieved if he were dead."

R.J. Corgan

"Not relieved," Gwen corrected. "Giddy, in fact. Elated. I'd even go so far as to say thrilled."

Kea blinked.

"Yes, of course I hate him." Gwen shrugged her shoulders. "But that doesn't mean I want him dead. Hating someone and spending the rest of my life in prison are two different emotional plateaus, not to mention two different sets of life goals. I have too many other things I want to do in life to let him ruin those too." She shook her head. "This isn't Cabot Cove, Jessica. There's no need to go hunting for suspects. It was an accident. This is the Kalahari. There's loads of things waiting to sting, bite, or eat you for supper."

"Sorry. I've been trying to not do this." Kea waved her hands in the air between them, "but I can't seem to help it. That spider. I just can't believe he'd be that careless."

Gwen nodded. "There are about a dozen ways out here to kill someone that would draw less attention than going after a spider that's probably never even ever bitten anyone." Catching Kea's sharp look, she expounded. "I Googled."

"Unless you shove your toe in its face, presumably," Kea corrected.

"Besides," Gwen leaned over the table. "If you're looking for someone who might want to kill him, you won't have to look far. Not here." Her eyes darted across the room. "*He* pretty much wants to kill all of us. I'll be checking my shoes every morning, I don't mind telling you." Gwen considered. "Not to mention my bras."

"What are you talking about?"

"Has no one told you? Seriously?" Gwen made a noise like a sheep being vivisected.

It took a moment before Kea realized it was the sound of Gwen laughing.

"Mani of course," Gwen whispered. "Addi was on his thesis defense. Mani failed, twice. I'm surprised he didn't whip out a gun and shoot him right then and there. It's happened before you know. Remember when a guy shot all three of his panel? That was at San Diego State. For a master's degree, for God's sake."

Kea turned in her seat to see Mani at the faculty table loading up his water flasks. One at a time, he filled them up with a flavor powder, shook the bottle, then moved to the next one, completely unaware that there was a woman sitting ten feet away, calmly accusing him of a homicide.

"Nothing wrong with a master's degree," Kea said, her voice filled with exasperation. "I had one, once upon a time." She wasn't eager to question Mani about last night's events. If *Anger and Fury* were a cologne, the man would reek of it.

"And what about Katherine?" Gwen mused.

"Jilted ex-wife?" Kea had already considered it, but the scenario seemed too obvious, especially for someone like Katherine.

Gwen shrugged. "With Addi gone, the position of Department Chair would become vacant. She'd still have to apply, of course, but there's no one more qualified."

"Nope," Kea said firmly. "There wasn't anyone caught on the cameras going in or out of the cabin during the last twenty-four hours at least. It's your classic locked-room mystery..."

"No, it isn't." Gwen protested.

"I know, I know," Kea sighed. "It's not a room, it's a tent."

Gwen shook her head. "It can't be a locked room mystery if the victim isn't *alone*."

"Tamaya? Never," Kea replied defensively before realizing she hadn't given the possibility even a moment's thought. *She couldn't have. Could she?*

A staccato clapping filled the air.

Katherine stood at the end of the hall, hands on her hips. She gave the students a withering look, waiting impatiently until their chatter ceased. Tristan stood beside her, flinching under the stares of the crowd.

"We're headed out to the field in thirty minutes," Katherine announced. "Make your lunches and pack your bags in ten, or else the jeeps leave without you." Then she left, with Tristan trailing behind.

"Business as usual, it seems," Kea muttered as the students flitted around the hall, emptying trays and grabbing foodstuffs. They moved quickly, but silently. Sullen.

Grieving.

"There's nothing 'usual' about any of this," Gwen sniffed and shuffled off.

Kea looked over at Mani, wrestling with the desire to ask him a question. On the one hand, she hated talking with strangers, especially conversations where she had little to lead in with except, *'So, where were you last night?'*

In the end it was her stomach that managed to club her inner introvert into submission: if she wanted lunch, she'd have to pack one.

The faculty had their own preparation station, which smacked of elitism. However, considering the student station was slathered in peanut butter smears and dusted with drink powders, Kea decided that this was exactly the kind of elitism she could get behind.

The assortment of meats, breads, fruits, and vegetables on the faculty table were even better than yesterday. She went straight to the little dish of capers, although she had no idea what she was going to put them on. PB & Capers sounded a little too avant-garde.

Mani stood at the end of the table, packing up his pastrami sandwiches into little paper bags. His fingers were long and delicate, a contrast to his sinewy arms that disappeared up the sleeves of a dark cotton shirt. A necklace of white gold shone against the dark skin of his collar, hanging loosely around his sloping shoulders.

He was ridiculously handsome. Except, Kea reminded herself, for the chewing tobacco. On the entire ride back to camp the man had spit the residue into a used soda bottle.

She cringed at the memory, then took a stab at starting a conversation. "Do they ever put out something more…local? I mean, this is all amazing, but it's nothing I couldn't get back home."

"Sometimes Tshepo will surprise us." Mani sliced off some chunks of Muenster. "Usually though, he puts out what the students will eat. He doesn't like it when they leave things to waste. And whatever you do, don't ask him about peanut butter."

"Noted." Kea opened the jar and scooped out a dollop of the offending substance onto a slice of bread, then studded it with capers. "Life is too short not to try new things."

"Some things are okay to skip, including whatever that is." Mani grimaced at her meal as he finished wrapping his cheese.

Kea kissed her teeth with her tongue in frustration. He was stuffing the last of his lunch into his bag, putting away the silverware and was and about to leave. *The last time I hesitated, people had died. Damnit.*

"I just wanted to say," she began, "I heard about what happened with your Ph.D. degree defense, and I can sympathize."

Mani's body language changed in that instant, from swagger and sexy to still and tense.

She tried a different track. "Over the last few years, when Tamaya would tell me stories about these expeditions, do you know what struck me the most?"

He remained silent.

"Not once did a jeep break down. Not once did a trailer flip. Not once did a battery die…"

He snorted. "That's because I do my job."

Silence fell between them.

"Seven years." Kea said quietly.

A long moment of silence strung out between them, but he made no move to leave.

"Seven years," she repeated. "After comps, I did two years of research. Including writing up, the entire Ph.D. took me seven years." She blew out a breath. "I'll never get those years back. The nights, the weekends. Not to mention all the money I wasn't earning towards retirement…and I'm not through paying them off, not by a long shot." She had always thought she would be paying off student loans long after she was dead. Of course, it never occurred to her it could be *this* soon. She tried not to stare directly at the knife in his hand.

While Mani didn't reply, he wasn't interrupting her either, so she kept talking. "It certainly didn't have to take so many years, of course, but life has a way of moving on, both for the student, as well as the advisor." She waved a hand around the camp. "Seeing everything here working so well, you do your job. You do it very well, under less than ideal conditions." She paused. "I imagine you took the same approach to your thesis."

Despite the dangerous look in his eyes, she pushed one step further. "What did the panel say you did wrong? Why did you fail your defense?"

"The committee cited errors in my methodology…" Mani seemed suddenly weary, his shoulders slumping in resignation. He slipped the knife back into the block and went back to packing up.

R.J. Corgan

Kea frowned. She had hoped for plagiarism or negligence. "But that's something your advisor should have well…advised you on, long before the defense – I mean both defenses."

"Yeah, that would have been helpful." Mani tucked his water bottles into his pack. "I guess Addi had other things on his mind."

The tension between them seemed to have evaporated, so Kea reached over and picked up some water bottles. The stale taste of the warm water in the field yesterday had convinced her to try some of the flavor powders. "Did you file a complaint?"

"Well, you see there was one problem," he shouldered his pack, then held out a hand to stop her. "Don't touch that."

She looked down at the yellow green powder she was about to scoop into her water. "Why, is it dangerous?"

"God no, it's just disgusting, only Skellington drinks that. Anyway, the problem was that Addi was right - they were all right. They even gave me the chance to submit revisions."

Kea was confused. "Why didn't you?"

"To re-collect and reprocess new field data? It would take another two years."

"You don't seem terribly upset about this."

"You kidding? I was pissed. For four weeks I couldn't step foot on that campus without wanting everyone dead."

"And now?" Kea ventured cautiously.

"Now?" Mani blew out a long breath. "I don't have time for that. When we get back, I got a gig working with one of the major labs as an engineer. My starting salary is about twice what Addi's is." He laughed. "He was quite annoyed when I told him. And still is annoyed when I find a way to mention it nearly every day. Which is a great deal of fun."

After Mani left, Kea found herself staring at the array of flavors before her, bewildered as much by the selection as the quirks of academia. *How can someone put all that time into something and just walk away?* After all, she considered, isn't the relationship between a teacher and a student just like any other long-term relationship?

"How much happier would life have been," she asked herself, "if I'd just been able to walk away from Jason. Or Karen. Or Tommy…"

Convinced that the grape powder seemed to be judging her, she opted for cherry instead.

***

Over the next half hour, Kea and the remaining faculty played mother-at-large to the student horde. She made her way through their throngs, making sure they wore adequate sunblock and had packed enough water. She helped load the gear into the trailers and checked that the equipment boxes were secured, all the while fielding their questions about the status of Addi and Tamaya.

Since she was just as in the dark as the rest of them, she sidestepped their queries with the bland and useless phrase, '*I'm sure they'll be back by dinnertime.*' The suspicious looks she got in return reminded her that she was just as terrible a liar as Tamaya.

Short on drivers, Katherine drove the lead jeep, while the rest of the leads followed in their respective vehicles, including Kea. As she drove, she focused only on the fender of Katherine's jeep in front of her. Completely drained of energy, despite the glorious sights that she saw as they bounced and rolled down the tracks, she couldn't process any of it. All she wanted to do was take a long nap and wake up to discover that her friends were fine.

The caravan headed eastward, toward an older site further out on the pans. She lost track of how long they had been driving, although she did appreciate driving a field vehicle built in this century. The jeep her teams used in Iceland were purchased in the mid-1980s and had died several times, only reluctantly resuscitated by the university's mechanics, often using blunt force and the odd bent coat hanger.

The meerkat expedition had splashed out some serious cash on these vehicles. She played with some of the shiny buttons on the dash, discovering that not only were they equipped with heated and air-conditioned seats, but these babies could parallel park themselves. Not exactly a high priority in the desert, she reflected.

The students unloaded the gear while the other leads checked over the equipment one more time. With no Tamaya or Addi, and having never been to this site, Kea felt as useless as a spoon at a steak eating contest.

The students, for their part, dispersed in an orderly fashion, as if they were Marines going into battle. They knew their orders, their mission, and their duties. They collected their packs and assembled their kit under Katherine's steely gaze.

Kea found herself drawn to the field observation tent, a scruffy looking hexagonal structure of tan canvas and silver piping. Inside, she found Gwen working on a laptop wedged within piles of cables and random bits of gleaming tech. "Isn't this a little overkill for meerkats?"

"This was one of the first colonies that Addi studied, but their numbers have dwindled over the last few years." Gwen shook her head sadly. "They're probably not going to recover."

Not what I asked, but good to know. Kea's gaze lingered on the computer screen that displayed a virtual model of the colony. An image of the landscape rotated slowly on the screen. Little red flags marked the entrances to the meerkat's tunnel system. It looked like a cross between a virtual geological map and a very expensive arcade game.

Noticing her attention, Gwen tapped the screen. "This is built on your standard lidar base…"

"You blast the terrain with lasers," Kea translated. Common enough for geological work, but for meerkats? "To do what, exactly?"

"We create three-dimensional models of the terrain," Gwen waved a hand over the series of low rises and ridges that comprised the meerkat colony. "Which is pretty easy, given the flatitude."

"That's not a word." Kea rubbed a sheen of moisture off her brow. The heat of the day was already starting to take its toll and it was only nine in the morning. "At least, I'm pretty sure it's not."

"Then we merge the exterior terrain with the interior model of the tunnel using these gambits." Gwen stroked the head of the little robot on the table. It looked like a futuristic overfed hamster. Two belts encircled its body, each with four rubberized wheels.

Kea noticed that Sock lay abandoned on the table beside the droid. Maybe knitting wasn't Gwen's only true love.

"These beauties map out the interior space of the tunnels. You can watch through these." She handed Kea a pair of square shaped goggles. "I've got some data from last week loaded in there so you can virtually walk through the colony's tunnels."

Warily eyeing the stains on the rubberized edges of the goggles, Kea slipped the strap over her head. A vivid recreation of the meerkat tunnels was visible on the inside of the lenses. With the dramatic change in scale, she suddenly felt about five inches high.

"Use this to steer."

Kea felt Gwen press a joystick into her palm. With it, she found that she could experience a 360-degree view as the device replayed its journey through the short twists and turns of the burrows. A giant-sized meerkat appeared in front of her, causing her to yelp in alarm. The creature paused to sniff the gambit's camera lens before scooting around and out of sight. She watched it scamper away in the tunnel. Before it disappeared, she noticed a virtual sticky note hovering in the air. It displayed the meerkat's name, alphanumeric code and other facts including sex, age, and date.

"I guess it's useful." Kea removed the goggles. "If I ever needed to play *Meerkat Tomb Raider*..."

"We're using them to map different colonies in the area."

On Gwen's screen, Kea saw four colonies highlighted on the map. The colony closest to the lodge was picked out with a helpful giant 'Home' icon. That must be Genevieve's mob. Judging by the map, she could see Nikita's location and the new location they were working out of now. Another colony was labeled *'Boudicca'* and appeared half-in and half-out of the reserve boundary. *The one with the serious poacher issues.*

"We're trying to determine if there's a pattern to the tunnel's architecture, or if the structure is dependent upon strata. Although, in truth, the tunnels are fairly simple." Gwen pulled up four different tunnel designs. "Meerkats tend not to do well in confined spaces like zoos, so we're trying to investigate their dens to help alleviate stress factors."

"I don't think any of us do well in captivity." Kea looked away from the virtual colony to the real one sprawled out before them. "Hang on a sec, how do you connect all this? I mean digitally?" She pointed upward. "Is it a satellite connection?"

Gwen shook her head. "Can't afford that. The FaceGoogle balloons are overhead a few days a week, so we use a tower to connect to them when we can."

Kea squinted at the horizon but couldn't see a mast. However, the clouds were low, their dark forms scudding across the horizon. They could be hiding anything. Based on the geography, she guessed the tower lay somewhere in the middle of the colonies. "I don't understand why all this tech gets spent on these little guys."

"The truth? This is only research in the university that gets any money. And it gets a lot." Gwen shook her head. "All the other groups, like the tech divisions, just glom onto it because they know they'll get funded. Wouldn't be surprised if the Chemistry department starts developing a pill to cure male meerkat-pattern baldness."

"That's..." Kea weighed her question carefully, "not real, is it?"

Gwen considered. "The last paper I read focused on bacterial colonies in meerkat butt pouches." Noticing Kea's expression of disgust, Gwen added, "They turn them inside out to scent their territory. When it comes to research ideas, and if there is funding, nothing is out of scope."

***

The team spent rest of the morning documenting the meerkats cleaning their burrows, foraging for food, and babysitting their pups. The students weighed and measured then weighed and measured again. A dozen times over.

Kea wandered between the different groups of students as they worked and squinting at the instruments, nodding knowingly. Mostly, she watched the meerkats.

She also watched Katherine, from a safe distance.

The woman spent most of her time with Gwen, filming 'micro' documentaries, short two-minute segments to put up on social media. The contrast between the terse, impatient woman ordering Gwen around and the warm, smiling personality she inhabited when filming the segments set off all sorts of alarm bells in Kea's mind. She did not like people who could change personas so easily. It made them impossible to read.

It wasn't just for the camera, she noticed. Admittedly, Addi was...*is*, Kea mentally corrected herself, Katherine's ex-husband, but Kea thought Katherine would display a little bit of concern. Instead, Katherine seemed all 'business as usual.'

Kea helped the students out whenever she could, but for the most part, they knew more about what they were doing that she did, so she hung back and took photographs. At one point, while watching the little meerkats bask in the sunlight, she found herself sighing.

"What's the matter?" Gwen asked.

"If glaciers were half this adorable," Kea postulated, "people would have demanded climate change be stopped a decade ago."

"Tell that to the polar bears."

"Touché," Kea replied sadly. It was only then that she noticed Gwen was walking and knitting at the same time. Kea was impressed. Walking was often challenging enough without trying to produce a cardigan. Or Sock for that matter.

At lunchtime, they convened at Tristan's station and Kea used the opportunity to observe Katherine as she ordered a student to get her more water. Kea found could not read a single line on the woman's expressionless face.

"It's like trying to lip-read a shark," she muttered.

"You say the strangest things," Tristan observed.

She hadn't noticed him sitting beside her. She edged her bum over on her rock with the pretext of giving him more room, while really trying to put more distance between them. "That's word-for-word what my therapist said."

"You have a therapist?" Tristan asked around a mouthful of potato chips.

Kea had to avert her eyes. The man did not close his mouth when he spoke. It was like watching a Muppet eat a bowl of cereal. Bits of chips flew everywhere. "Had," she corrected. "It was a long time ago." Last month, to be precise. Said therapist had suggested that perhaps that Kea living out of her university office might not be the healthiest way of handling her breakup with Zöe, her ex-girlfriend. It was at that moment that Kea decided to find another therapist.

"Did you have any luck with the images?" Tristan asked.

She wanted to give him credit for changing topics, but she guessed it was more out of lack of interest in her mental state than in deference to her personal issues. "Nada." Kea stabbed a straw at her juice box in a futile attempt to pierce the foil seal. It appeared to be made of Teflon. Three more stabs only succeeded in denting the tip of the straw. "Although I wasn't sure what I was looking for."

"It can take a while to learn the training images." He tried to sound sympathetic. "Still, lion, hyena, snake…it's not a Mensa entrance exam."

"Thanks for that." Kea decided it was a great time to find a bush and deal with all the water she had been drinking. She made to get up, then realized her legs had fallen asleep under her and she found herself stumbling into a crawl. She clutched her pack for support and managed to pull herself upright. Like a cat, she glanced around to see if anyone had noticed.

"I can automate anything you want," Tristan said eagerly. "Can have the system send alerts."

Kea paused at the top of her wobble to squint at the gangly, broken comb of a man. "Say that again?"

"On your tablet." Tristan took another chomp of his sandwich. "Use the alert tool, the red thing on the top left on the map. Draw boxes around any areas of the colony you want to see, and it can either send you a live feed of just those areas, or you can set it to e-mail you when something moves or changes inside the frame."

She frowned. There was nothing in the future she wanted to see, not that she knew of anyway. "Can you set it to look at the past?"

"I'll have to change some settings, but yeah." He seemed to think it over. "Send me a map marked out with the regions you want. How far back? A year?"

Kea boggled the thought of having to review that amount of data. "How about just the last month or so?"

The man nodded, seeming happy to help, although completely disinterested in anything other than tackling a technical challenge. Perhaps she had misjudged him after all.

"That's not right," Katherine swore from inside the tent. She came out holding a pair of binoculars. "Cameras four and seven went down."

"Meerkats with wire cutters?" Kea couldn't help herself.

"Poachers, more likely." Katherine let the binoculars swing down to her chest, so she could shield her watch from the sun's glare.

Kea sat up in alarm.

"What is *that?*" Tristan frowned at his own watch.

A series of harsh alarms went off across the group like a cry of angry birds. Several of the students headed for the shelter, while the others slung their packs and started loading up the trucks. Katherine sprinted back inside the tent with four students following at a trot.

"What's going on?" Kea asked Tristan, only to discover he too had sprinted to the tent.

Before she could follow, Tristan and the students re-emerged carrying two of the black-shelled containers. They placed the cases on the ground about twenty feet away from the group. Releasing the clasps, the students opened the lids and fell back to a safe distance. Tristan reached into one of the cases and withdrew a chrome cylinder about three feet in diameter. His fingers played over the edges for a moment before he threw the device into the air. With a faint whine, it hovered ten feet off the ground as it traced an irregular path of a cross in the air. Then, the sound pitched up an octave and the cylinder sped off into the distance. Tristan withdrew another device from the second box and repeated the procedure.

Kea knew a drone when she saw one, but she had never seen one quite so sci-fi before. She couldn't conceive how they could even be aerodynamically possible. *It was like watching a bumble bee go into warp speed.*

"What on earth is that?" she asked.

"They were donated. Our imagery team sent them over." Tristan squinted into the sun as he watched their progress. "They map the soil types, geology, as well as keep an eye on the colony."

"Who is this donor?"

"Dunno."

"You could find a lot more with that than just meerkats." Kea frowned, trying to remember the geology of the area, wondering what else they might be looking for.

"Like what?"

"Lots of things," Kea said. In her mind, she rattled off a number of possibilities, including uranium, rare earth minerals, likely locations for gold deposits. Africa was quite literally a gold and diamond mine. *Not out here though. Just miles and miles of evaporites. What could they be looking for? It's just salt...*

Kea edged her way through the mass of students that pressed against the flap of the tent. Inside, Katherine was seated at a desk with two mini laptops, their cases colored the same chrome as the strange globes. Katherine took the controls of one, while Tristan took the other.

Kea found herself wedged against Gwen who was watching from the sidelines. "Any ideas?"

Gwen nodded at Katherine. "She mentioned more heart rate spikes."

"Poachers?"

"This is different." Gwen shook her head. "Meerkats...I think. Going by what Tristan said, the geofence alert went off earlier."

"A rover?"

"Not a single meerkat," Katherine answered. "This is an incursion."

"Territorial dispute," Tristan translated. "This colony's gotten too big for the food supply." He pointed to a screen that displayed the trackers against the background of a topographic map. "We've been watching them for a while. Looks like they've finally decided to make their move on their neighbors. Nearly the entire colony is out there."

On the screen, Kea could see the tags move as two distinct groups dived into one another. Each time they intersected, the tags shifted in a coordinated manner, like a shoal of fish. Through the drone's cameras, they watched the devices speed across the desert, Katherine and Tristan navigating them to the skirmish.

"They might be too late." Tristan pointed to the screen where the glowing points of light were swarming around, and within, each other. "It's going to be over by the time we get there."

"Nearly there." Katherine shoved the joystick forward.

As the drone descended, the ground on-screen grew larger. Kea could see the meerkats now. Their tiny tails were held high like swords as they darted across the sands, their backs arched. A few meerkats sat back, away from the fight, their eyes on the sky. They had noticed the drone, but seemed to ignore it, not raising the alarm.

Tristan's drone reached the fray. He positioned it at the other side of the pack. Katherine reached over to another terminal and flicked a switch.

Kea gaped as the tracker points, complete with meerkat ids, appeared on the video feeds, matching the location of the meerkats exactly in real time, causing her to whisper, "That's insane."

The cameras zoomed in, allowing her to discern the individuals as the two mobs of meerkats swarmed each other, racing across the sands and darting between clumps of grasses.

"That's Nikita." Tristan pointed to one of the leading animals. The matriarch's label was highlighted in yellow.

Kea scanned the other mob and was surprised to see a name she recognized leading the charge. "But that's Genevieve!"

"Nikita's been scouting round the edge of Genevieve's territory for weeks now." Katherine adjusted some of the controls to get a better resolution.

"There's so many..." Kea breathed.

There must have been thirty meerkats per side, rushing toward each other in a wave. The animals leapt at each other, sometimes one-on-one, other times swarming smaller groups or individuals. The camera slipped in for close-ups.

Kea wished they hadn't. It was a vicious thing to see. The sharp claws and needle-sharp teeth stabbed and bit into the throats of their opponents. They tore into each other, the little bodies twisting and squirming as they struggled for dominance.

It was all over faster than she could have imagined. Thankfully. Nikita's group beat a hasty retreat, slipping away through the grass, some of them chased by Genevieve's mob.

Genevieve, Kea noticed, appeared unscathed. *Good news for Genevieve, not so good for Hazel.*

Cletus was not so lucky.

Tristan pointed out his prone body on the camera. Even as Kea started to process the loss, the lens panned out further, displaying another limp form on the sand. Other meerkats in Genevieve's mob were lying down, panting heavily, many licking their wounds.

"Will the rest be okay?" Gwen sounded horrified.

Katherine, clipboard in hand, was busy taking notes. "Some will, some won't. Tristan, can you replay the attack again from a different angle? I want to make sure we got footage of Nikita, see how bad her wounds are."

Not wanting to see another frame, Kea stepped out of the tent. The heat slapped against her face, almost causing her to step back inside. The sky was filled with tall clouds, their bases merging together into a mass that cast long shadows that seeped across the floor of the pan. Despite the heat, she felt a chill travel up her spine causing her to clasp her arms about her chest. "Looks like a storm's coming."

"I hope so," Gwen commented. "It is the rainy season."

Kea turned to see that the woman had followed her out.

"You okay?" Gwen asked.

"I wasn't quite expecting that." Kea nodded to the tent and images of the bloodied animals tearing at each other's throats. "Plus," she began, then stopped, determined to think of something else. Something other than Addi. Her eyes caught the shimmer of the drones, tiny specks floating in the distance. "I still can't believe those things."

In Kea's experience, she had to fight for every penny to keep her expeditions afloat, often using her own money to supplement when things got tight. To see such expenditures on these little guys made her mind ache. "I mean, don't get me wrong, they're cute and all…"

"Meerkats are a big business," Gwen chuckled. "Don't knock cute."

Before Kea could reply, the tent flap was yanked sharply back. "You better get in here," Tristan called, sticking his head out of the tent. "We found out what happened to the rest of the cameras at Boudicca's colony."

Kea trailed behind Gwen as they slipped back inside the tent and looked at the screens. "Jesus." Gwen breathed. The rest of the team were similarly swearing, some even averting their eyes from the displays.

Stepping closer, Kea squinted, trying to make out what had so alarmed the others. The drone was hovering over a warren, the irregular pattern of dark gaps highlighting the tunnel entrances. There were no sentinels, she noticed, just lots of meerkats, all laying on the ground.

It was not until she noticed the birds tearing into one of the furry little bodies that she processed that they were all still, that they were all dead.

"Even the pups?" Tristan asked.

Tristan shook his head. "Can't tell."

"What the hell happened?" Gwen sounded stunned.

"Disease?" Kea offered. "Infection?"

Katherine shook her head. "Infections don't smash cameras. We lost all the new ones we installed three days ago. And whatever happened, it was fast." She headed outside, barking orders. "Kea, stay here and watch the students. We'll be back in under an hour. Tristan, record everything, then get the drones back safely. Gwen, use the gambits to see if you can find the pups in the tunnels. Mani, you're with me. Call the wardens enroute, let them know-"

"Already on it." Mani, who had been lounging at the jeeps, had his satellite phone pressed to his ear.

"Better get the students doing something useful," Gwen muttered. "Okay everyone," she called to the group. "Get everything packed up. We're done with field collection for the day."

Kea watched in dismay as the teams started packing everything away in the remaining jeeps.

***

"Poachers," Katherine announced upon her return. She had gathered the staff around one of the jeeps, away from the students. "They used poison and then guns. Didn't even bother to hide it." She held up a picture on her phone showing a discarded box of what looked like rat poison and a cracked plastic bowl with the crusted remains of a gray pasty mixture in it.

It took her a moment to process that someone had just deliberately killed a whole colony of meerkats. "They just left that?"

"They wanted us to find it." Tristan sighed. "Or rather, for the reserve's wardens to find."

"You moved it?" Kea was mortified that they had touched the evidence.

"This isn't CSI," Katherine chided. "We already sent them the photo with the coordinates of where it was. Besides, we couldn't leave it there in case some other animals…"

"But," Kea sputtered. "Why would anyone do this?"

"Cameras." Katherine, although exhausted, sounded almost bored. "They took out the cameras, but they knew we'd replace them, so rather than constantly keep taking them out…"

"…Just 'take out' what we're here to watch instead," Gwen finished. "That's horrible."

"With no more colony, no more cameras…" Tristan said sadly. "They can hunt whatever they want without anyone watching now. They took everything, all the cameras, all the equipment."

"So," Kea looked around the circle of faces in the tent. "What do we do?"

There was a long moment of silence. No one met her eyes.

85

"We don't *do* anything," Katherine said softly. "We leave it to the wardens. We're biologists, not NYPD."

"Didn't you say that the cameras that went down were outside the reserve?" Kea pressed. *You have all this monitoring equipment, there must be some way of catching them...*

"Boudicca's brood expanded the colony outside the preserve boundaries..." Tristan trailed off. "But like she said, all the cameras have been taken out."

"But what about their outfits, their fitbits? They've got cameras on them, right? We can identify the people who did this."

Gwen placed a hand on her shoulder.

Katherine's phone rang. She glanced at the others then stepped away to take the call.

"Only Genevieve's and Nikita's colonies had the trackers on them. This week we were going to put them on Boudicca's team." Gwen paused. "It's almost like they knew..."

"Kea." She turned to see Katherine striding back toward them. Her face was completely devoid of emotion. She walked directly to Kea, who stepped back in alarm. Kea was even more surprised when the woman gently took her arm with her free hand. "She wants to talk to you," Katherine said, holding out a sat phone.

Pressing the receiver to her ear, Kea found that her hand was trembling. Part of her knew she didn't want to hear the news. *Because then it will make it real.*

Chapter 6 – Pour Decisions

DINNER THAT night was a somber affair.

Kea's mother had loved phrases like that. At the age of sixteen, Kea totaled the family car, as well as a small chunk of a Taco Bell, and her mother, on hearing the news, admitted to being, 'A *tad* disappointed,' and then calmly dealt with the insurance companies. Emotions, as her sister was always fond of saying, were things that happened in *other* people's families.

The reaction of the staff and students to the news of Addi's death was similarly subdued. Already unnerved by what had happened to Nikita's colony, word spread quickly among the students. While they were not outright bawling, tension hung in the air as they struggled to handle a new, almost alien, emotion. They still chatted quietly and even occasionally looked up from their phones, but the mood in the main hall was grim. Although the events of the day had no observable effect on their appetites, Kea noticed. She had barely been able to salvage the last brownie from the buffet. The pudding trays were similarly scraped clean.

She managed to find an empty length of table and sat with a cup of coffee, settling down to help get some of Tamaya's work done, and prevent herself from freaking out. Receipts from the weeks' purchases that needed to be entered into the accounting system sat on one side of her laptop while and a tray of biscotti occupied the other. She focused on her work while the herd clattered their utensils and murmured restlessly. The other staff had retired to the AV tent to confer on a plan of action. Not having a stake in the decision, nor any research to sacrifice, she had offered to supervise mealtime and play the role of responsible adult, although she would be the first to admit that adulting had never been her strong suit.

When she and the rest of the teams had returned from the field, Tamaya and the others had been waiting for them. Aside from a long, weepy hug, Tamaya offered little more than she had imparted over the phone. The infection, the seizures, the stress, all of it had been too much on Addi's heart. His body remained at the hospital, while Tamaya returned to camp to collect their things and hand over the running of the expedition. Then she would finish dealing with Addi's remains before heading back home.

Knowing Tamaya's desire to at least give the impression of keeping it together in front of the students, Kea had settled for the hug, but before she released her, Kea whispered that she was welcome to crash in her cabin that night.

Right now, however, Tamaya had a lot on her mind. They all did. *Should they stay or should they go?*

It was no small decision. In addition to the sheer logistics and costs of moving the equipment and supplies out of camp early, there were also the students to consider. Changing flights, getting picked up by family members, even just transporting them to the airport would be chaotic. They had the jeeps to shuttle the students and all their baggage to the bus stop at the nearest village to catch a bus that only ran once every three days. When the rich vacationed here, Kea had been informed, they just used their private planes. Undergraduates attending a state university had no such luxuries.

There was a good deal of money tied up with the decision, not to mention the loss of research, prestige, and of course, there was also the safety of everyone at the camp to consider. She was glad to not be the one having to make that decision for a change.

"Been there, done that," she whispered into her coffee. If it were up to her, she would have them all pack up and go. "And never look back…"

"Few people who come here ever do." Tshepo's baritone caused her to spill her coffee. "At least, most don't. Addi was one of the few."

Kea had been so consumed by her thoughts, she hadn't noticed him sitting beside her. He helped clean up the spilt coffee, daubing at the table with a wad of napkins.

"Shouldn't you be in the tent with the rest of them deciding our future?" Kea asked.

"Not my call." Tshepo rested his hat on the table and ran a hand across his scalp. "How are you holding up?"

Kea spent the last twenty-four hours consumed with worry about Addi and Tamaya, the students, the expedition, what she was going to do when she got home, the fact that she no longer had a home. It never occurred to her that anyone might be worried about *her*.

"Fine," she replied automatically. Then added, "If 'fine' is a word one uses to describe someone who is incredibly worried, stressed, and at the end of their rope, then I'm fine. Come to think of it, all my mother ever said was 'I'm fine,' so I'm beginning to think she may have needed a great deal of therapy-"

"I've known Tamaya for a long time," Tshepo cut in before she could continue rambling. He turned his hat over and over in his hands. "She'll be okay. Eventually."

Rationally, Kea agreed with his assessment. Tamaya would be okay, although it might be a very, long time from now. She decided to change tracks. "Did you see anything last night? Anything odd?"

"Aside from an old friend dying from a horrible bite?"

"Yes, well, aside from that." Searching her memory, Kea could not remember where Tshepo was before the chaos erupted that night. Nor Katherine for that matter. Nor Carter. Nor Tristan, nor…she frowned. *I need to make a list.*

"Nothing out of the ordinary, if that's what you mean." He leant back in his chair and let out a long, tired sigh. "Now, lions, that's the way to go."

She found his alternative scenarios to be just as gruesome. "How do you mean?"

"A scorpion sting takes hours to really do a lot of harm," Tshepo expounded. "Most adults can survive, although it can depend on the species. Children, or someone Addi's age, that's a different story. Even the snakes aren't deadly, not really. An adder bite will hurt like hell, yeah. A Cape Cobra, now that could kill you, except we have anti-venom in the stores."

Kea had heard all this before, yet something tickled in the back of her mind. "And yet Addi gets bitten by the one thing that's never bitten anyone ever before and by something we don't have an antidote for."

"It is odd." Tshepo sighed. "Then again, so was he."

Silence filled the air between them.

"What do you think they'll decide?" Kea looked out into the darkness. The AV tent was still illuminated. Dark shapes seeped through the canvas as people paced within.

"I imagine," Tshepo said, "that you're all going home. Only sensible thing to do."

"Thank goodness for that."

"I've helped close down this expedition several times before," he added. "If all the staff and my family help, we can probably get the students out by tomorrow, but as for taking down and packing up all the equipment and vehicles, that's going to take a while. Two days at least."

Kea let that thought settle about her shoulders. *If the spider wasn't an accident, did one of us put it there or did one of the poachers? Did they want the expedition shut down completely? How would they know who to go after? Do they have a man on the inside?*

She found herself nervously eyeing Tshepo, then shook herself free of the thought. Due to the web series, Addi was as famous as a rock star, there was no need for an inside man to know who to kill. *Spiders to the left of me, poachers to the right.*

Still fascinated by the nebulous ghosts projected against the wall of the AV tent, she turned her attention to the desert beyond the main hall. Backlit from the flickering torchlights, her own shadow appeared to be pressing its head against Tshepo's in an intimate silhouette. She waved her hand at their elongated forms. "I wonder what they're talking about."

Tshepo seemed to take the question seriously. "There are a lot of superstitions that our shadows continue as representations of our souls, long after our bodies die."

Kea stared out into the black veil of night, itself an invisible wall created by the limits of the camp's bright lights, separating them from the cold desert. "I wonder if Addi's out there, watching over the meerkats."

"If he is, I hope there aren't any undergraduates out there snogging," Tshepo joked, knowing as she did that students tended to sneak out after sunset for some privacy.

"Worried Addi'd scare them?" Kea chuckled.

"I knew him when he was single and footloose," Tshepo smiled. "I'm more worried he'd try and join in. Addi was the same way when he was married to Katherine. Tamaya wasn't the first student he messed around with, that's for sure."

Kea was prevented from discovering more information on Addi's exploits by the return of the leadership team. They filed into the main hall, Katherine at their lead. Tamaya trailed at the back, her expression unreadable. A hush fell across the hall as they stepped up beside the faculty table.

Katherine cleared her throat. "We're going to make arrangements to get all of you home, as soon as possible. Effective immediately, we're shutting down the expedition."

As Kea expected, a chorus of groans filled the air, but she was surprised to discover that she felt the same as the students. On the one hand, her Spidey-senses were telling her to get the hell out of Dodge. However, the thought of getting back on a plane after only having spent three days in Africa, grated.

Katherine rattled off the rest of the details, but Kea barely listened. She processed bits of it. The jeeps would ferry back students to the village in the morning, while one vehicle would remain to take down the equipment from the field sites.

Much like Kea, the students had already tuned out, pecking away on their phones, informing parents, and the rest of the world via social media. *Who knows, maybe the poachers are following us on Twitter…*

As the students dispersed, she stepped through the shifting mass of bowed heads and grumbling couples to speak to Tamaya. It was only when she reached the end of the hall that she discovered her friend had already left. *No doubt*, Kea thought, *to avoid all the students. All the questions. All the reminders.*

"It's going to be a very long night," she muttered.

"It's going to be a very wet night." Tshepo stood behind her, waiting for the students to shuffle out.

Honestly, can't a girl just talk to herself anymore? "What do you mean?" she asked instead.

He looked up from his phone. "Radar shows rain on the way."

"It is the rainy season. Hence the name, one would imagine." She frowned at the consternation on his face. "Are we in trouble?"

"No trouble." Tshepo shook his head slowly. "But tomorrow, you'll be with me. Taking down the equipment. In the rainy season."

Kea cursed. She should have paid more attention when Katherine read out the duty roster. "I zone out for one second…"

"Have a good night." He waved cheerily as he slipped out of the hall. "Better get some sleep."

"I can't tell anymore," she sighed as she watched the last of the students shuffle off into their encampment. "Is that a blessing or a curse?"

For once, no one answered.

***

Receipts in hand, Kea found Katherine working on her laptop inside her cabin. While the piles of folders and printouts appeared to slosh and flow across the desk, the chaos only seemed to accentuate Katherine's outfit, a slick little number composed of tan slacks, sharp leather belt, and a loose white blouse inside a fitted navy jacket.

Kea bet that if there had been crumbs on the desk next to her coffee mug, they would be neatly arranged into little ornate arrows designed to draw attention to the woman's blouse. Now that she looked more closely, Kea realized Katherine was wearing a half-cape, half-sweater. She struggled to remember what it was called. A quarter cape?

Stepping closer, Kea made an effort to ignore the posh outfit, or at least tried to read the label without staring outright. "How are you holding up?"

Katherine acknowledged Kea's arrival with a wave of her hand and continued clicking away with her mouse.

Curious, Kea peeked at the screen. Histograms and figures of meerkat biodata spun as Katherine's delicate fingers updated the spreadsheet.

Her question ignored, Kea didn't know how to proceed. Was the woman angry? Depressed? She finally settled for the direct, honest approach. "About what happened to Addi, I mean."

"Oh that." Katherine waggled a hand a little dismissively. "Awful, of course, but more so for Tamaya for having to handle the arrangements."

Ah, I forgot about the other possibility: Relief. "I take it then, that you're not too upset," Kea remarked.

"I haven't missed him since the alimony and child support checks stopped, if that's what you mean," she replied candidly. "I'd find it hard to believe if he left me in the will, or even some kind of insurance payout, but aside from that…Rocco should get something. At least, Addi promised he would."

Kea had forgotten about Katherine's son. Tamaya rarely spoke about Rocco, leaving Kea to dig up half-forgotten tidbits. He had to be nearly thirty now, working in L.A. running odd jobs, and had been arrested more than once for driving under the influence. Needless to say, Rocco was not spoken of much at work. *The joys of parenting.*

If she were honest, Rocco seemed the most normal of the trio. She couldn't imagine how awkward it must be for Katherine to have to show up every day and work in the same office with, not only the man who left her, but with the woman he left her for. "It must be difficult..."

Katherine, no doubt wishing the conversation to end, turned on her. "Look, I read about all your 'adventures.'" The woman used her pinky fingers to mark the air quotes in such a condescending way that Kea wanted to bite them off. "But if you're asking me if I had anything to do with his death, then please spare me." She paused. "I'm not likely to have done it, as I'd be the prime suspect. I'm not an idiot."

Kea's mouth hung open in surprise at the outburst. She held out the stack of papers. "I just came to give you these, not interrogate you as a murder suspect." *I was going to do that tomorrow,* Kea added silently. *After breakfast.*

Katherine didn't apologize but sighed heavily. She rolled her chair back and crossed her arms over her chest. "Having been married to someone for fifteen years, having spent so much time with them, and then having it all end so quickly. It feels...wrong somehow."

"In what way?"

Katherine gave her a quick up and down glance. "Never been married, I take it." It was not a question and Katherine did not wait for a confirmation, which Kea found mildly insulting. "It's hard to spend a decade with someone who is your best friend, particularly once you've had children..." she stared listlessly at the monitor. "When they betray you, you will find that you'd much rather watch them suffer than just let them die quickly. Just murdering them would be so...unsatisfying."

Kea blinked. The casual tone of Katherine's words sent a chill up her spine.

"Mind you," Katherine continued, "at least this will end the ongoing travesty."

"Sorry?" Kea asked, finding her voice.

Katherine gestured at the papers on the desk. "He was good. Very good. Brilliant," she conceded. "For a while. But his last few of papers were dire, to be honest."

"Was his data incorrect?" Kea asked, wondering how they would have gotten through the publishing process at all if they were that terrible.

"Not wrong, exactly," Katherine considered. "The data itself is fine. It's just the hypotheses are so…uninspired. In my day, Addi would have been embarrassed to have even submitted them."

Feeling as if she had heard enough Addi bashing for one day, Kea turned to leave, but paused. A question had been burning in her mind since the first time she'd meet the woman, and this might be her last time to get an answer. "Why do you stay? Working in the same office as Addi and Tamaya, I mean."

"I love San Diego," Katherine replied simply. "It's my home. I love Africa. I love my research. Addi and Tamaya took my family away from me, but I'll be damned if I let them take those away too."

***

After a quick visit to the kitchen for a snack, Kea made a last stop at the equipment store. She almost felt guilty as she opened the cabinet and used the light of her phone to rummage around the boxes for more sleeping meds.

Almost.

The thought of facing yet another endless night staring up at the ceiling was enough to overcome any qualms of getting caught. It was worth the risk to spend a blissful night unconsciousness. Besides, she doubted the few pills she had would cut it.

Alex, I'll take "What are Things an Addict Says," for five hundred.

When the light switched on, she lost her grip on the case and very nearly control of her bowels. Thankfully, only bandages and boxes of medication spilt onto the floor.

"What the hell do you think you're doing?" she found herself asking Carter just as he asked her exactly the same thing.

"What the-" They chorused in unison again.

Carter held up a hand.

"Fine." Kea bent down and started to gather up the supplies, feeling shame flush her face. The packages of bandages kept slipping through her fingers. It was like trying to pick up a pile of dry leaves. "I was just..." she stuffed what she could into the case, before making another attempt. Frustration bubbled up in her throat, forcing tears out of her eyes. "I just needed something to help get through the night."

She felt his hand on her arm. She couldn't keep her hands from shaking and it pissed her off that he could feel her tremble.

"You could've just asked," Carter said, his tone irritatingly reasonable. "But if you keep stealing them, there won't be any left."

"Stealing?" Her outrage fueled a knee-jerk reaction of disgust. Even if that was exactly what she was doing. "I've only taken a few. That's hardly going to-"

"A few?" Carter cut her off. "They're nearly all gone. I checked when I was putting this place back together."

"What are you talking about?"

Helping her re-assemble the contents of the kit, he picked up the boxes of sleeping medication and shook them upside down. "See? Nothing."

"They were there the other night." Kea knew she was pushing the limits of credibility, but in this instance, she had honesty on her side. "I swear it." Now that he mentioned it, she remembered that she'd found the sealed capsules at the bottom of an opened box. She had just assumed the other boxes hadn't been opened yet. "I think."

Carter considered her, then shrugged. "If it wasn't you..."

"Anyone can get in here," she pointed out. "It could have been anyone." *Literally*, she reflected. *Students, faculty, any of the staff.* "They're just sleeping pills. Is there anything else missing?"

Carter frowned, then dug around the boxes for the inventory sheet. He began to pull out the contents of the medical kit, fumbling with the clipboard.

Growing tired of playing the spectator, Kea took the sheet from him and called out numbers as he checked the remaining medications and supplies. Everything else, including the two doses of snake antivenom, was present and accounted for.

As they packed everything back up and closed down the equipment store, Kea asked, "You know what?" Carter raised a querying eyebrow. "I think I'm kinda glad there aren't any pills left."

She flicked off the lights and picked up her bag. "There's so much strange crap going on, I don't think I want to be knocked out any more. Who needs sleep anyway?"

She saw an expression of something other than disapproval cross Carter's face. True, it was pity, but the change was a relief.

He sighed, then reached into his jacket and pulled out a couple of tiny plastic bottles. "I think you need these more than I do."

***

Tamaya was not in her cabin. Concerned, yet wanting to respect her friend's need for space, Kea settled for leaving a note on her porch, then returned to her own cabin.

She sat on the porch with her feet tucked under her behind and looked at the cabins. The students seemed to have settled down for the night. A few of the smokers stood in a circle near the edge of darkness, tiny little red embers twirling as they gesticulated with their hands in sync with their conversations. The rest of the camp appeared to have already gone to sleep, as all of the porch lights were off. Kea turned hers off as well but remained sitting. Waiting.

She finished the first bottle of vodka, keeping the second for Tamaya.

After the first hour passed, she finished that one as well.

It was another half-hour before her new friend appeared.

She opened the Tupperware she had taken from the kitchen and took out one of the shiny, white objects. She broke the egg apart and tossed the bits into the darkness. Hazel stepped out of the shadows, following the trail of crumbs. Her steps were tentative at first, then more confident as Kea tossed more food. It was not long before the little meerkat was sitting on Kea's knee, taking bits of egg out of her hands.

"I think Addi would approve," Kea said. "At least for tonight."

Hazel was fixated on the remaining bit of egg.

"Here ya go." Kea tossed the last chunk of egg into a cardboard box that she had wedged at the base of the doorway outside her cabin. "There's room at the inn, if you like."

A light patter-pat-pat echoed from the darkness as the first of the rains began to fall. With little else to do, Kea sat beside Hazel on the porch and watched as the storm hit.

Chapter 7 – Dodgy Dongas

SOMETHING WAS wrong.

Kea's eyes snapped open, sleep forgotten. Her cabin was flooded with shades of gray. It was still early morning, but the usual blaring beams of sunlight were absent. Instead, rain clouds smeared the curtains with pallid blurs, stretching ashen shadows across the floor. Her eyes adjusted slowly to the gloom. The floor, covered with scattered clothes and field equipment, held irregular shadows and vaguely ominous forms. Without her glasses, she couldn't make out a thing.

She heard a quiet movement above her head.

It was a rustling sound, just outside of her line of vision.

She was not alone.

She lay motionless, barely breathing. Terrified.

Run for the door?

After the previous night, she reasoned that she would probably fall over herself trying to get out of the sheets and the netting.

She gasped, a tiny sharp intake of breath.

She had not noticed until now. There wasn't any netting. She definitely remembered crawling into bed and draping the gauze behind her, even tucking it underneath the mattress.

Someone had untucked the veil, leaving the side of the bed wide open.

Walls, I love walls, who the hell builds a hotel in a desert with lions, tigers, and snakes without some goddamn walls?

She heard the sound again. Whatever it was, it was large.

In the room with her.

Next to her.

Kea's mind raced to think of anything in her possessions she could use as a weapon. She hadn't packed her rock hammer. At home, she carried around a handy bottle of mace in her purse; however, out here the strongest thing she had was a jar of *Gray Poupon* she'd nicked from the kitchen.

Not helpful.

Think.

The sound came again. Closer now.

Very slowly, she tilted her head upward.

It was then that she saw it, an alien form, dark, and oblong. Its shadow trailed through the jumble of cups and combs that littered her bedside table.

Kea reacted without thinking.

Snatching up a coffee mug, she slammed it down as hard as she could on the creature, again and again. Cold brown water flew through the air in an arc, spattering the white linen sheets. She heard a satisfying *crack* as the mug fragmented. Still holding the handle and part of the cup's base, she pounded and pounded until the thing fell to the ground. She stomped on it repeatedly, screaming obscenities, her raged fueled by pure panic, *"Die! Die! Die!"*

"Kea! It's okay." A voice broke through the stomping. "You killed it."

Who the hell?

Kea threw herself across the room, away from the thing, away from the voice. Her foot snagged on the strap of her pack and she tumbled to the ground in a heap.

"Although what you have against hairbands. I have no idea."

Tamaya. Tamaya had been in her bed.

Kea pulled herself up and approached the lumpy form beneath the covers, pausing to scoop her glasses off the floor.

Tamaya pulled her head out from under the sheets, her hair a tangled mess that static electricity had spiked into a halo. The greasy sheen of her forehead and the light brush of a moustache on her lip spoke of someone pushed beyond exhaustion and in desperate need of a shower.

"I waited up for you," Kea stammered, attempting to return to rational conversation as adrenaline throbbed in her veins. "I must have dozed off. How are you?"

"At least one of us got some rest." Tamaya slumped back on the bed and pulled a pillow over her face. "I'm fine."

"Liar," Kea whispered.

"I'm fine. Go back to sleep." Tamaya pulled the covers back over her head, effectively ending the conversation.

Kea really had no idea what to say. She felt useless and awkward, like a left-over Halloween decoration at Christmas. She had so many questions. *Was she by Addi's side when he died? Was he in agony? Was he peaceful? Was he awake? What about the body? The funeral? The expedition?*

Not knowing where to begin, and not wanting to put her friend through the strain of having to answer any questions, she did as she was told and crawled back into bed. She gathered up the covers around them and hugged Tamaya.

At first, Tamaya remained rigid in her embrace, but soon she was trembling, sobbing against her chest. As Kea listened to her friend grieve, a selfish thought ran around and around in her head:

Everywhere I go, people die.

***

Kea slipped away around seven in the morning. Tamaya was still asleep, buried under the comforter. The gray clouds outside refused to let any rays of sunlight through and the usually sandy paths were caked with mud as the rains continued to batter down in waves.

After so many days of intense heat, the cool touch of the water on her skin and the stiff breeze in her hair was invigorating. The slate color of the sky and the drops that pelted her face reminded her of Iceland, minus the lions, desert, and meerkats, of course. Maybe it was that familiar sensation, or maybe it was the fact that she had slept properly for the first time in ages, but she felt as if she could accomplish something again. She quickened her pace, enjoying the sensation of hope.

We're going home.

The students appeared to share the same sense of excitement. They dashed between the main hall and their tents and the coffee crowd that usually gathered under the porch eaves was absent. The line for breakfast still looked formidable, however. Despite her craving for caffeine, she was drawn to the loud noises coming from the vehicle bay.

The structure was little more than some aluminum roofing nailed over tall posts that offered protection from the sun's rays. Beneath it were parked many of the jeeps and the large campers that held the science labs. Several of the equipment trailers had already been unhitched from the jeeps and swapped with luggage trailers. One still had its clamshell lid propped open and it juddered as Carter lobbed bag after bag inside it.

She nodded hello, then climbed into the trailer and started arranging the bags. He paused long enough for her to assemble some sense of order, then began her tossing more bags that she stacked in the case like firewood. When they finished, they attempted to close the cover, but even with Kea sitting on it, they couldn't get it to latch properly. Finally, they gave up and she helped him secure a tarp over it, strapping it tight with elastic cords. They stepped back to survey their handiwork.

"I feel like Dagwood made more architecturally sound sandwiches." Kea said at last.

"It just has to hold until the village." Carter sighed. "Then it's the bus's problem."

"Are all of the students even going to fit?"

He shrugged. "No idea. Worse case, some students spend a night or two in the village."

Kea remembered the ramshackle little village where she had arrived on the bus a few days ago. It seemed like weeks. While it might have held around six hundred people or so, she couldn't remember seeing anything resembling a Ritz...or a Red Roof for that matter. "That's going to be...interesting."

"They'll be safe." Carter said firmly. "Tshepo said they'll be taken care of."

They stood together in silence, listening to the falling rain before heading back to the main hall for breakfast.

"Do you know if Addi suffered?" She found that her voice was cracked and raw, the words barely intelligible. She swallowed and tried again. "At the end, I mean?"

"Massive hemorrhaging, organ failure..." Carter's voice trailed off. "At least that's what Tshepo said." He cleared his throat and stepped away to double-check the straps. "Funeral's Saturday. Tamaya said he wanted to be buried in Botswana."

Kea frowned. "Can he do that? I mean, as an American..." *Does death have citizenship?*

Carter shrugged. "She and Addi agreed on it a long time ago, apparently. Got all the permits years ago."

"I can barely plan meals more than a week ahead of time, let alone where I'll be buried someday." She listened to the rhythm of the rain drumming on the metal roofs.

100

Just a taste, Carter informed her, who had looked at the forecast. The real storm would come through sometime in the afternoon. Kea found she was looking forward to it. *You can take the girl out of Iceland...*

"A deadly spider that never bites," Carter said eventually. "What are the odds?"

"That's my line." She studied him out of the corner of her eye. "What was your master's in again? Biology?"

"Botany, among others."

"Others?"

"I have...oh, let's see." Carter counted on his fingers. "I think I'm up to eight now"

"Eight...what?"

"Master's degrees."

"I thought you only had one," she blurted, although she meant to ask, *Why would anyone need more than one?*

"Well, one from UC Burlingame," Carter admitted. "The others, well, once you start a law degree and your student loans crack the two hundred grand mark, you can either pay them off or just keep going."

"You just keep going?" Kea asked, dubious.

"'Til I retire. As long as I'm enrolled in a university."

"And you'll never have to pay for any of it?"

"Some would argue a lifetime of homework is payment enough." Carter smiled. "I'm actually on this trip because after high school I started out as a paramedic and have kept up my certifications. Although I'm still a lawyer by day, adjunct faculty member at night. And, on the other nights, still a student."

"What research are you doing out here?"

"Aside from the bullfrogs?" He shrugged. "Getting a degree in Quaternary geology. I need pollen samples for my thesis."

Kea frowned. She hadn't seen anything that resembled a core sample on the expedition. She added it to the list of things to check on. Her thoughts returned to Addi. "You're not an arachnologist by any chance, are you?"

"Spiders freak me out." Carter shook his head. "Life happens, I guess. Flush and move on."

Kea considered that and reflected on her life of late. "I think I want that on my tombstone."

R.J. Corgan

***

When it was time to retrieve the field equipment, Kea spied Tristan in the driver's seat, so she opted for the relative safety of the back. Carter climbed in beside her, forcing Tshepo to join Tristan up front.

Studying the back of Tshepo's Stetson, Kea couldn't shake the feeling that they were on their way to rustle cattle. Or at least rob a slow-moving train.

As they pulled out of camp, she saw Gwen and Katherine usher a group of students into one of the field vehicles. Tshepo had some of the staff helping drive some of the other jeeps, but it would still take two trips to get everyone out. Given the options of carting around disgruntled undergraduates or collecting field gear in the rain, Kea was happy with her lot. Not that she'd been given a choice.

Ten minutes later, as they sloshed and heaved their way along the rain-soaked track, Kea felt her breakfast rising in her throat. The beginnings of a migraine began to seep into the edges of her vision. She gripped the door handle, silently urging the vehicle to move faster.

They had left without waking Tamaya. She would be furious when she realized she'd been left behind, but they reasoned she needed the rest. Besides, they weren't conducting research, they were just taking everything down.

As they drove, Carter held his cell phone in front of his face, the speaker on full volume, chattering in his native German. An elderly woman, possibly his mother, was on the other end, talking just as loudly.

Kea tried giving him her well-practiced *'There's a place in hell for people like you'* scowl, but he appeared oblivious. Of course, there was also the possibility that people could not tell her scowls apart. *I should hand out a spotter's guide.*

She was just about to 'accidentally' slam Carter's phone onto the floor with a well-placed elbow, when the woman's voice sputtered, then abruptly cut out. Carter tried redialing but the *'no signal'* icon persisted on his screen, much to Kea's relief. "Must be the tower's down," he muttered. "Or else the Facegoogles can't get the signal through the weather."

Reaching the first site, Kea found the process of striking everything relatively straight forward. Anything portable got chucked into the back of the jeep. The remaining equipment, mostly cameras, solar panels, and sensors, was checked to ensure that connections were secure, lenses were grime-free, and data was downloaded. Once the equipment was checked, she roamed the area and picked up any bits of rubbish, then took photographs to document how they left the site.

By the third site, she had found three pairs of sunglasses and two cell phones. Scratched and scarred by the blowing sands, she guessed they had been left by previous expeditions. Over her many years of fieldwork in Iceland, she had lost count of how many pairs of sunglasses she had left behind on the black sands. *Is this how archaeologists in the future will be able to track scientific expeditions, by their discarded sunglasses? If aliens ever visited us, did they leave behind futuristic Ray Bans'?*

"Kea!" Carter waved at her from a marker, calling for a new survey nail. She jogged back to the jeep and spent the next hour fetching and carrying. As she worked, the spatter of mud on her trousers crept higher and higher. By the time they piled into the shelter of the jeep for lunch, they were all drenched.

They waited impatiently for to Tristan turn on the engine. "What did one raindrop say to the other?" He asked, knowing he had a captive audience. "Two's company, but three's a cloud. Get it?"

He continued to tell terrible jokes as they ate their lunches, their damp rears soaking the seats. Kea devoured her peanut butter banana sandwich. Her tepid coffee tasted better than anything she would pay for at a roaster. Despite the warmth, she found she was trembling. At her request, Tristan cranked up the heaters another notch.

"Right, one last site," Tristan muttered around the nozzle of his camel pack, "then back to strike the main camp." He slipped the jeep into gear and turned back onto the tracks, windshield wipers straining under the volume of water. "Anyone staying in the capital for a few days after the funeral or is everyone heading straight back?"

Kea hadn't thought about what she was going to do after this expedition, let alone think about the funeral. She'd come here partially to help Tamaya, and partially to escape from her own problems. *And look how that turned out.*

Her train of thought was broken by an excited "Woo hoo!" from Tristan as the jeep slithered down an embankment into a drainage channel. Normally dry, there was a fair amount of water in it, but nothing the jeep couldn't handle. They shot across, causing a huge spray of mud to fan out from either side.

She watched as the ripples were quickly subsumed by the rising waters. The Makgadikgadi Pan was just one of a series of ancient lakes, left dry as a result of changing climate conditions. Essentially, however, they were driving in a channel that fed into a giant depression, which naturally led her to the question of, "How recently was this channel last active?"

Tristan looked at her via the rear-view mirror. "Say what?"

"The water, where does it all go?" she repeated.

She could tell from his scrunched eyebrows that he didn't understand her question.

"We're in an old lake bed," he provided uselessly.

"I know," Kea sighed. At this moment she really didn't want to try to lecture him on the glacier floods in Iceland, how many used the flash floods in the arid southwest United States as an analogue to understand the deposits. In her mind, while the pans were completely different landforms, the rainwater still had to go somewhere before entering the basin. "I know, but what about the –"

Everything happened so quickly.

Tristan's shoulders twitched. The spastic movement was followed by a sickening groan as his eyes pinched shut and his hand clawed at his throat. The jeep slewed, turning into the rushing water as his other hand yanked the wheel. The current began to tug at the rear of the jeep.

Lunging from behind, Kea tried to grab the wheel, but the sharp slap of her seat belt threw her backward. Another jolt jerked her head sharply back as the jeep lurched forward, presumably caused by Tristan's foot slamming onto the accelerator.

Carter swore as his phone dropped to the floor and slid under the seat.

Tshepo grabbed the wheel, attempting to right the vehicle, but overcompensated. The jeep leaned at an alarming angle, wobbling for a moment in the rising channel. Tristan's face turned beet red, and a terrible gurgling sound bubbled up from his throat.

"Get his leg off the pedal!" Kea shouted. She pounded on Carter's arm to get his attention. "He can't breathe!"

Confused, and holding on to the 'oh-crap' handle with one hand, Carter tried to reach Tristan. The jeep lurched as the wheels first caught, then lost traction in the shifting mud. The wheels spun furiously as the engine revved out of control.

Releasing her seatbelt, Kea reached around the gearshift and grabbed at the fabric of Tristan's pants, trying to lift his foot off the pedal. It was no good. His spasms kept his legs locked in place. The passenger side tires bit into the gravel beneath them just as the channel waters swelled, lifting the driver's side of the jeep up into the air.

She gasped as time seemed to fall from one moment into the next in slow motion.

Then Kea felt her head slam against the ceiling of the jeep. Her vision flared with a blinding white light. Then she was choking, gagging on a mouthful of water. Then another.

She felt a strong hand yank her head up, lifting it out of the water. Blinking, she realized that she had not hit the ceiling. Rather, the roof was now the floor. The vehicle had overturned.

Water flooded in from all sides. She lifted her head above the rising waters and pulled herself into a sitting position.

She heard an unearthly groaning sound. She could feel it vibrating through her entire body. The current, she realized, was moving them, scraping the jeep's roof along the channel floor. The sensation of movement was enough to snap her out of her stunned haze and she reached for the door.

Whether from the weight of the water or the crash deforming the frame, she couldn't force the door open. She pounded on the window in a panic, but she only succeeded in bruising her fists. She slid back along the seat and braced to kick out the glass, but a hand on her shoulder held her back. The same hand, she realized, that had pulled her out of the water.

"Kea!" Carter waved at her. She registered the shattered windscreen, Tshepo pulling Tristan's out the passenger side, and more importantly, Carter's open door. "Come on." Tugging at her arm, he pulled her through the wall of water that was still pouring inside the jeep. "Get out. Now!"

She splashed through the rising water, her knee thumping against her pack. Grabbing the door frame, she pulled herself out of the vehicle. The strength of the current knocked her feet out from under her. She felt a strong embrace around her waist and then a heave. She gasped in surprise. Tshepo had tossed her on top of the vehicle.

Or rather its belly, she corrected herself as she struggled to find footing on the undercarriage. She stumbled, falling on her back. She stared at the dark sky overhead in a daze as lighting flitted from one cloud to another. *When did the storm get this bad?*

Shouts drew her back to reality.

Tshepo and Carter were pulling Tristan clear of the vehicle. Even as they handled him, she noted that his boy was lifeless, a limp rag doll that dangled between them. A six-foot three, one-hundred-eighty-pound rag doll, Kea realized as she struggled to shift Tristan up onto the jeep's undercarriage.

Carter leapt up beside her and began performing CPR. Clambering onto the jeep after him, Tshepo was soon assisting.

Kea looked across to the channel edge. It wasn't far, less than a few feet, and the water was not more than waist deep, but it was rising quickly. She watched as streams of their belongings washed out from the jeep and trailed away downstream.

Call for help!

Frantically, she checked her pocket. Nothing.

Her phone was in her bag.

In the backseat of the jeep.

Kea swore.

Tristan wasn't responding to the CPR efforts. Knowing there wasn't anything she could do, she took a firm grip on the edge of the front wheel well and swung herself back into the channel wash.

The water was warmer than she expected, but the power of the channel's flow was enough to make her cry out in shock. Her feet could touch the ground, but she was worried that another shift could trap her beneath the jeep. Keeping a tight grip on the door, she trailed freely and reached in through the windshield that was now facing downstream. As the items drifted out of the jeep, she caught as many as she could, and tossed them up onto the undercarriage.

She managed to save a couple packs, as well as three small equipment cases, a thermos, and a laptop case before she was dealt a glancing blow to the head by a survey rod. It made a gonging sound as it struck her temple. It should have hurt, but the cold, or perhaps the adrenaline, numbed any pain.

It took a full three seconds for it to sink in that she could be skewered by another of the drifting rods. She abandoned any hopes of retrieving the phone and clambered out of the water.

Ripping open the zippers on the rescued packs, it took her a moment to register that Carter and Tshepo were both motionless. She saw they were kneeling by Tristan's side, their heads bowed.

The body was limp and pale. His eyes were open, staring lifelessly upward.

Kea didn't need to ask.

Another groan juddered the soles of her feet as the jeep shifted. The force of the water lifted the jeep above the channel floor, causing Kea to fall to her knees. They were floating freely now, adrift in the channel and picking up speed.

As panic threatened to overwhelm her, Tshepo and Carter moved away from Tristan and started picking equipment out of the packs, grabbing the memory devices and other expensive looking gear. The all-business, salvage-what-we-can, attitude helped her regain focus.

It almost made her forget about the sight of Tristan's body and the agonized expression that was carved into his face. She found herself fascinated with the flecks of foam that had bubbled around his pale lips. *Not helping.* Kea turned away, retching. Wiping her chin, she saw the detritus the men had abandoned, discarded bits and bobs they'd deemed nonessential.

"There!" Carter pointed to a constriction in the channel up ahead where several boulders protruded above the waterline. With some careful hopping, Kea considered, they could make it to the riverbank. The tricky part would be the dismount.

She realized with rising disgust, that they'd have to leave Tristan behind.

Carter pulled on a pack stuffed with data cores, each component still sealed in their respective pouches. She understood why he was trying to save them. The tech they could replace, but not the data. Not everything had been uploaded to the cloud yet. Assuming the water hadn't already ruined them.

R.J. Corgan

Noting their weight, Kea didn't offer to help. *I'm not going to die for meerkat data.*

The sound of rushing water grew louder, signaling the increasing turbidity in the channel ahead. If they didn't get off the jeep soon, she knew there was a chance it could roll again at the next constriction or topographic drop.

Kea spared Tristan one last look. As horrible as it sounded, it was not as if his body would be washed out to sea. Instead, once the floodwaters joined the ancient lake bed, the water would dissipate, leaving the body stranded. More concerning, however, would be the condition the corpse would be in by the time the waters receded, if they couldn't get to him before the wildlife did.

"Come on," Carter shouted as Kea crawled in the opposite direction. "Get ready to jump."

"One sec." She scooted to the edge of the jeep and snagged Tristan's daypack. She suspected that whatever had killed Tristan wasn't natural and she was damned if she was going to let the evidence get away. She half-crawled, half-stumbled back to Carter, her knees buckling as the vehicle swayed in the current.

"What the hell?" Carter asked.

Kea shook her head, intent on the boulders racing toward them. The jeep was rotating slowly now, making it even more difficult to time their jump.

They spread their weight out in a line along the undercarriage, in case their dismount unbalanced the vehicle. She found herself in between the two men, as if they had both silently assumed that she might not be able to be the first to jump or that she would need their help.

Although annoyed at their presumption, she was glad. The throbbing in her head was deafening and every motion made it worse. Adrenaline was starting to shunt the pain out of the way, thankfully, but she was losing her footing and the lenses of her glasses were blurred by beads of water and sweat.

The boulders loomed in front of them.

Tshepo jumped first. As he leapt, the jeep, now unbalanced, rocked alarmingly. Kea felt a shove from behind her as Carter pushed her into a run. She sprinted toward the rushing water that was now a torrent of thick, black raging froth.

Terror made her hesitate, betraying her in that last important moment as her unconscious mind made the decision between certain death ahead and a *maybe* certain death if she remained on the jeep. *Ican'tIcan'tcan'tcan'tcan't-*

She sensed, rather than processed, Carter running up behind her, then alongside her. His hand yanked her belt and they finished the leap together, Carter rotating mid-jump to throw her ahead of him. Tshepo, still securing his footing on the rock, turned and reached for her.

Realizing she wasn't going to make it, she found herself absurdly mentally cursing her high school Phys Ed teacher for letting her skip gym. *Damn you, Mr. Gillette. Why were you so nice?*

Her foot slammed into the boulder, but with too much force. The awkward landing and the slippery surface of the wet rock caused her to rebound and she started shifting sideways toward the water. Crying out, she tried to fall onto the boulder, her arms thrashing desperately.

She felt a sharp jolt. Tshepo had hooked her elbow with his own. She clung onto him with both hands, until a terrible weight from behind forced her down on her knees, dragging her toward the water.

It was Carter.

Unbalanced by her added weight, he had misjudged his own jump and had slammed into the rock. One of his legs had slipped into the water and she could see the floating cobbles battering him as he struggled to find purchase. His hand, she noted, was still lodged in her belt.

They hung that way, frozen in an untenable tableau, as Tshepo tried to balance the weight of all three of them from his precarious position. Kea felt herself being torn in two, her feet slipping out from under her. Carter screamed as the turbid waters buffeted him, the current yanking him with fitful jerks. Despite her blurred vision, Kea saw Tshepo's legs tremble, his boots subtly shifting. *He's not going to be able to hold us. We're going to take him down with us.*

For one horrible second, she considered removing her belt and letting Carter fall into the water to save herself. To save Tshepo, she amended, lamely attempting to rationalize the decision.

After a moment the vile thought passed, replaced by the realization that this was all too familiar. The rushing water, the screams of terror, the numb certainty of what Fate was about to deliver. *I've been here before.*

Kea risked a glance downstream. The jeep was now floating on its side, probably overturned by their dismount. Tristan, or rather his body, was nowhere to be seen. Reds and blues swirled in the muddy brown waters as bits of equipment bobbed up and down, caught in an eddy between the rocks before they were swept out of sight.

She turned back to Tshepo. His teeth were bared, his eyes wide, and his arms trembling with the strain. He might not have the strength to haul them back up, she thought, but he sure as hell was not about to let go.

Not again.

She reached down and grabbed the handle of Carter's backpack. Letting out a shuddering breath, she looked back to Tshepo, gently shook her head and let go of his arm. Tshepo staggered backward, free of their weight, an expression of panic flashing across his face.

Then he was gone.

Her head dunked under the water and the current tore her feet out from under her. Dark, silty water rammed its thick fingers into her eyes and down her throat, soaking her boots until they felt like globs of solid concrete.

Kicking frantically, she broke the surface. Kea spit out a mouthful of water and saw Carter beside her, screaming, the rush of the torrent drowning out his words. Still connected by his pack, the currents began to spin them in the channel, circling faster than she expected. Her legs and chest slammed into cobbles and branches in the roiling water. Thrashing as hard as she could, she steered them toward the rocks, and then, with a final desperate *heave*, they slid into an eddy.

Their arrival was brutal. A boulder slammed into her shoulder, threatening to dislodge her grip on Carter. Discarded bits of cardboard, Styrofoam, and empty cases propelled by the current, knocked against their heads, further disorientating them.

Try as she might, she couldn't get grip on any of the boulders. She grazed her knuckles as she cast about, trying to use their slippery shapes to lift herself above the rapids and get a better view, to find her target. She cried out in relief when she spotted it. A survey staff had lodged between the rocks and the force of the currents had wedged it in place. She dove at the staff and threw her free arm over it. It bowed under their combined mass but didn't break. She bellowed a primal scream as she managed to lock her elbow around the bar.

She held on for dear life, hurling obscenities at the sky as the water and rocks pounded her. She lobbed one insult after the other at the heavens, each word dragging her from one moment to the next, as she tried to make it through just one more second, one more word, one more breath, one more profanity. The sharp pressure of the pole under her shoulder grew from an ache to a stabbing pain as the weight of Carter's thrashing body threatened to pull them both downstream. *Just please let me hold on, just please-*

The weight of Carter's body suddenly vanished.

Panicked, she spun around, expecting to see Carter being washed downstream or worse, submerged and gone forever. Instead, she saw Tshepo crouched on the rocks by the channel edge, his massive hands hoisting Carter out of the water.

"Yes!" Kea yelled, slapping the water in triumph. Wrapping both arms around the pole, she pulled herself toward Tshepo's outstretched hand. With his assistance, she was able to hop from rock to rock until they both collapsed on the embankment, taking huge, gasping breaths. The rain continued to pepper their faces, but the drops seemed insignificant now.

She watched the carcass of the jeep drift further downstream, wondering what would have happened if they had not jumped.

If Carter had not thrown her off.

He sat beside her, his head between his knees, spitting up water. He looked wet, bruised, and haggard, but otherwise unharmed.

Am I?

She spat up a runny wad of mucus onto the sand. Gingerly, she traced her scalp with numb fingers. She identified several lumps she estimated to be about the size of coconuts, but there didn't seem to be any traces of blood. Her left ankle ached, but she was still able to flex it. Her chest had taken a pummeling, yet deep breaths did not bring stabbing pain, indicating no broken ribs, although she wouldn't know for sure until she got to a hospital. *So much to look forward to.*

Unlike poor Tristan.

Tshepo sat in silence, watching them both with concern. It was then that she remembered Tshepo's expression when she let go and fell back into the water. The level of shock on his face surprised her. *I didn't know you cared.*

Carter, his coughing fit finished, tried to pull the pack off his back but failed, groaning in pain. She crawled over and helped slip the straps off. The pack was intact, but as she watched him extract the battered contents, she doubted anything contained on the drives would be salvageable.

Reflexively, she touched the straps on her own back and breathed a sigh of relief – the slight weight of Tristan's camelback was still there. It was the thing that might provide answers about what happened to him. *Or rather*, she thought, *who killed him.*

Chapter 8 – Surprises

THEY ABANDONED the road, hoping that they could get back to camp faster by cutting across the plain. Looking back, Kea wished they hadn't.

"This reminds me of that time I hiked to Angel Falls in Venezuela," Carter paused to yank his foot out of a particularly deep patch of mud. "The water there falls more than three thousand feet straight down, with a good deal of it evaporating before it hits the ground…"

Kea zoned out as he talked. She knew what he was trying to distract them, but she had too much on her mind. *Who could have wanted Tristan dead?* Assuming, of course, that he had been murdered and didn't just have some sort of medical condition that he didn't tell anyone about.

Wouldn't be the first time, Kea thought, remembering how one of her volunteers slipped into a diabetic coma on the glacier and nearly got them all killed. *Just one of these days I'd love to find a body, in a library, with a knife in their back. Sounds so much easier.*

"…a team of Brazilian ninjas were supposed to shuttle us across the border at night in a Ford Fiesta, but one of them insisted on being paid with a Rueben sandwich of all things…."

As Carter continued rambling, she eyed him nervously. *Did he put something in Tristan's water?* Carter certainly had access to all the medical supplies. As a biologist, he also may have known which spider to catch and how to find it. *But why? What would he gain by killing Addi?*

"…which sounds like a great bargain, but then you have to think, where are we going to find Worcestershire sauce at this time of night?"

She knew so little about this man who seemed to have spent so much time traveling the world, about his connections, about what might be lurking in his past. His stories made it seem like he was made of money, however, he had mentioned a massive amount of student loans. For all she knew, he could have other loans. It always stunned her how content people could be to rack up massive amounts of debt just to keep up appearances. *He doesn't seem the type somehow. But could he profit somehow from their deaths? Even so, why poison Tristan and endanger himself? Bad timing or classic double bluff?*

They crossed a region marked only by gray scrub, the terrain more salt than sand. Indeed, few animals seemed to live in this area, and others only passed through if absolutely necessary. *If they were being hunted, for example.* Kea stopped in her tracks, stunned at the tableau before her.

"I mean, who wouldn't consider a Croque-monsieur a fair trade? Hardly worth trying to crush my windpipe. Ninjas can be so temperamental..." Carter broke off abruptly as he took in the carnage.

Tshepo raised a hand to stop them from approaching the bodies. Four giant carcasses lay in the mud, their gray hides slick with blood, their faces butchered. *No,* Kea corrected herself. *They were mutilated.* For some reason, carving out their tusks meant gouging out half of their skulls. Or perhaps the poachers had just done it for fun.

Kea couldn't even identify the bodies as rhinoceroses, not at first. She was too overwhelmed by the violent red that had soaked into the sands and the discarded chunks of skull and brain. Bloodied pulp was the only thing that remained of the creature's necks. Steam rose from the bodies to mix with the light rain.

The acrid smell of a charnel house burned the back of her throat.

One of the rhinoceroses shifted slightly, as if trembling. She began to move toward it, not knowing what she could do to help, but she had to do something. Tshepo grabbed her arm, grunting.

She paused. The animal's back was toward them, but there was definitely movement. There it was again, just behind by its shoulders, near its belly...

Oh.

She saw them now. Hyenas, partially hidden from view, lunged and tore into the rhino's belly. Their attacks caused the corpse to judder and shift as they gorged on the feast within.

Resisting the urge to vomit, she followed Tshepo's lead and moved slowly and quietly as they skirted around the bodies and up a small incline.

Joining Tshepo on the crest of the hill, Kea was surprised when he urged them on into a jog. "We must get back," he growled. "Now!"

She stumbled after Carter, struggling to keep up as the mud pulled at her boots. "What's the rush?" Kea gasped. "They're not chasing us."

Carter descended into the hummock, but paused, poleaxed. Then he sprinted out of sight, yelling, "My research! My frogs!"

Kea stumbled a few more feet and then saw it. Hidden in a wash were the poachers' vehicles: two abandoned pick-up trucks. While free of water, the base of the channel was filled with supersaturated mud and the vehicles' tires were completely buried in the muck. Tracks on the other side of the embankment marked where the poachers had presumably climbed out and continued on foot.

Then it clicked.

The poachers' tracks, she realized, were headed straight for Mack Camp. Tshepo had sent away most of the staff with the students, leaving the camp, the ATVs, and jeeps unprotected, as well as their samples and data.

Tamaya!

Her friend was still asleep, possibly alone, and in great danger.

Despite her injuries and exhaustion, Kea found herself pelting across the mud and sands. Even running at full tilt, it took another ten minutes before they reached the camp's perimeter.

They were too late.

The sight of the little bodies scattered across the colony dropped Kea to her knees.

It was a massacre.

Some of the meerkats had been gassed. Some had been shot outright. Genevieve's body was easily identifiable, her head twisted into an unnatural position. Her leg had been shot, Kea judged, then her neck snapped.

There was no value to this, she thought. She stumbled around the carnage and ruined cameras looking for a living soul. There was nothing for the poachers to gain by this murderous act other than to send a message. *Leave and never come back.*

R.J. Corgan

Tshepo beckoned them away from the meerkats, waving them toward the main camp. She trailed behind the others, still stunned by what she had just witnessed.

They entered the camp warily, winding their way through some temporary storage tents. Taking shelter behind a pile of old tires and discarded bits of fencing, they watched for any indication of the poachers. The camp, however, appeared devoid of life. After a quick huddle, Tshepo headed toward the vehicle storage area.

Kea watched as he moved from one building to the next, using each as shelter. Once he was safely out of sight, she and Carter crossed the main courtyard in a mad sprint, collapsing in a heap in her doorway.

To Kea's immense relief, the cabin was empty. So too was Tamaya's.

Then another thought struck her. *What if they had taken Tamaya away with them?*

"Sat phone," she barked. "Now."

Carter nodded in agreement.

"I meant," she said as calmly as she could, "Where are they kept?"

"Ah," Carter said as realization dawned. "I've got one in my lab."

They headed back toward the vehicle storage area and were just crossing the entrance to the main hall when Tshepo caught up with them. "They came for the ATV's," he said wearily, his face devoid of emotion. "They took eight of them, plus some tanks of gas. There's two left, but they slashed the tires. Will take me some time to replace them."

"Any sign of Tamaya?" Kea asked, dreading the answer.

Tshepo shook his head. "The others are on the way back from the village." He held up his radio. "They'll be here soon. They're having the same issues with the flooding on the roads."

A numbing sense of despair gripped Kea's mind. The quiet around them felt unnatural. It was so still, so empty. Then another thought struck her. "What about your staff? Did they flee? Could Tamaya have left with them?"

"It's possible," Tshepo conceded. "If there's trouble, and no guests, they have orders to get somewhere safe." He turned away, thumbing the talk button on the radio.

116

"I'm gonna get the sat phone," Carter said, "and check on my frogs."

"Just wait a second," Kea chided. "We packed up everything in the AV tent and moved it to the trailers, which are locked. We can't be certain that the poachers have all gone. Let's wait for Tshepo, then we'll check the whole camp together. Maybe Tamaya and the others are holed up in one of the cabins."

Carter nearly twitched with impatience but relented. "They better not have touched Beatrice."

"How did we not see them coming?" Kea snapped. "There are sensors everywhere!"

"They took out the tower." Carter tapped at the darkened screen of his watch. "No connections, no signal. Then just smashed all the cameras they could find. I bet if they did find the AV stuff in the trailers, they probably trashed the hard drives for good measure. We back up the servers here in camp to the cloud every night at least…"

Tshepo rejoined them and reported on the fate of his staff. "They're safe. They left when they heard the poachers coming. They're on their way back now, but Tamaya isn't with them."

No, no, no, no. Kea fought down a cloud of panic that threatened to overwhelm her. "Sat phone," she repeated. "Let's get the wardens on this, if she's out there, they can help." *And if they can't, I'm grabbing an ATV and changing the tires myself.*

***

The trailer with all the AV equipment and lab tech was safe and secure, including Carter's frogs. It seemed that Tshepo's assessment that the poachers had only come to the camp to steal the ATVs was correct. Nothing else had been taken or stolen. *They must have been in a hurry to get out with their gruesome trophies.*

Something about that bothered Kea, but she couldn't put her finger on it. Her mind was still consumed with how to find Tamaya that found it impossible to concentrate. She couldn't look anywhere in the camp without seeing the bodies of the massacred meerkats.

Carter convinced her to sit down and eat something while they waited to see if the wardens could get a helicopter up to help with the search. She acquiesced, acknowledging that her body was on the edge of exhaustion. She grudgingly ate the plate of fruit put before her and popped one of the ultra-high caffeine drinks the students seemed to

117

live on. If she had to chase after Tamaya, she was damn sure she was gonna have enough strength to thump someone when she found them.

After downing three cans, Kea was so wired, she could feel her pulse throbbing beneath her toenails. "I can understand the rhinos," she began. "I mean I can't, but I see the money option, which is beyond stupid, by the way. I can even maybe understand that getting Addi out of the picture might scare us off, although I can't work out how they would have done it. I can even see why they did this..." she waved at the tiny lifeless bodies lying on the sand and found she couldn't finish that sentence. "But Tristan? He's dead...why would anyone-"

"Dead? What the hell are you talking about?" They turned to see Katherine standing behind them. Her field trousers and boots were splattered with mud and her sleeves were rolled up, revealing the taut sinews of her forearms. Her hair, dark with rain, was slicked back into loose curls that Kea had only ever seen in advertisements for designer salons. This woman looked amazing even after a hurricane.

Part of Kea hated Katherine. Another part of her wanted to know the woman's brand of conditioner.

The other team members trickled into the main hall. Carter broke the news of Tristan's seizure, cause *as yet unknown*, and the slaughter of the animals by the poachers. Despite Gwen's request to evacuate and nuke the site from orbit, Katherine shook her head.

"We got the students out, but the main road is completely washed out right now. Dongas are everywhere," Katherine said, referring to the gullies formed by the flooding. "It will be fine once it dries out, but no way we're getting across now, especially with the trailers."

"Trailers are overrated," Kea said emphatically. "I'm with Gwen on this one. I say we leave the equipment and scarper. Come back with the rangers and large volumes of weaponry that I usually spend my spare time lobbying to have outlawed."

"We're not going anywhere," Katherine said sternly. "We've called for help, we sit tight. Tshepo, you said eight ATVs were taken, is that correct?" Tshepo nodded. "Well, we don't know how many poachers there were. It's possible Tamaya took one herself before they arrived. If not, and if they did take her with them, then there's *nothing* we can do." Katherine stressed the word, staring at Kea. "If we try, we could just make it worse."

Kea glared back defiantly but said nothing. She reasoned that it would be easier to sneak away if they thought she had accepted the decision.

"Right." Katherine turned to them one by one. "Mani, check the remaining vehicles and see if any of them have been damaged. It could be possible that they didn't want us to follow them. Check everything, including the tanks and see how much fuel we have left. Carter, Gwen, Kea, help Tshepo stormproof the main hall and the cabins. He can show you where the storm walls are. We need to make sure this site and our supplies are secure. We checked the weather when we were fueling up in the village and it doesn't look good. The main storm is on its way." She turned back to Kea. "If we don't hear back from the rangers in thirty minutes, and if they can't get a helicopter up in this weather, then, if there's enough vehicles, we'll all take an ATV and check the fields sites. In *pairs*, not alone."

Kea felt her nostrils flare. Katherine's plan was a good one. *Damnit.* Kea nodded, the need to challenge Katherine fading. Besides, given that she'd just pounded three drinks, her bladder had other priorities at the moment.

"Finally," Katherine continued, "I need someone to volunteer to help take care of the colony. We must remove the bodies. We can't just leave them there for other animals to consume. Not to mention the impact on any children viewing the webcasts, should any of the cameras come back online."

As they dispersed, Kea followed Tshepo to the storage tents and helped set up the storm walls. The original Camp Mackenzie was meant to support guests during fair weather. The billowy sheets that comprised the walls, and often ceilings, weren't a match for a severe storm. While annual precipitation in the region could typically be measured in the millimeters, the recent changing weather dynamics, as well as the additional wiring for electronics that guests had come to expect, meant that the refurbished Mack Camp design had to incorporate waterproof linens and removable panels.

While undoubtedly an ingenious design, it became readily apparent that Tshepo didn't have the first clue how to install them. Fortunately, fifteen minutes of several frustrated attempts to secure a panel, the rest of the staff returned and were able to help them assemble the panels properly.

Job done, Kea was jogging toward the vehicle stores to steal an ATV, 'pairs' be damned, when she saw Carter and Katherine walking slowly through the colony. They were stooped low to the ground, their hands gloved, reverently collecting the tiny carcasses and tucking them into plastic bags.

Kea found herself drawn to them, overwhelmed by sadness. These creatures had spent their lives trusting people and yet their fearlessness wound up killing them.

Carter handed her a pair of gloves and a biohazard bag and before she could fully process it, she was kneeling beside a corpse. The industrial bag fluttered in her hands. For some reason, placing the body of this wild, adorable, and fierce creature into something as clinical as a plastic bag seemed obscene. *I don't think I can do this.*

It was then that she noticed another, larger body. Leaning closer, she saw it was the broken form of the meerdroid, half submerged in mud. She'd forgotten that Katherine had mentioned that she'd gotten one of the units working. *Was its video feed stored in the same folders as the regular cameras?*

She turned to ask Carter but saw that he was riveted to the spot. He was staring at something behind her. Covered in mud and soaked to the bone, a figure stood at the edge of the colony.

Tamaya.

Even at this distance, Kea could see the ruin on her friend's face as she took in the devastation. In the span of forty-eight hours, Tamaya had lost her lover and now her research and proxy-family. Despite the relief of knowing her friend was safe, deep inside, Kea felt something burst and she began to sob uncontrollably.

Chapter 9 – Amphibious CSI

FOR KEA, a shower was life's pause button.

Inside the cocoon of the warm jets and mist, she was left alone with her thoughts. Unlike sleep, she could emerge refreshed, ready to face the day. When she had a complex problem, she could retreat for a soak to puzzle out a solution. Other days she could curl into a ball and watch the water spiral down the drain and zone out.

Today was such a day.

She needed to organize her thoughts and try to make sense of the last few hours. Instead, she was numb, as if her mind was encased in packing foam.

Tamaya was safe. This, at least, provided Kea with an illusion of calm.

Discovering that she had been left behind, Tamaya had taken an ATV and followed Kea and the others. Worried that the cleanup teams might 'screwed up all my research,' she went from site to site, just missing them. The onset of the rain and formation of gullies had delayed her return to camp. Upon hearing the news of Tristan's death, Tamaya had not said a word. Instead, she secluded herself in her cabin.

The rest of the team adjourned to the main hall to debate how to deal with the latest threat, the oncoming storm. It had not been, as Kea assumed, a hurricane. However, Botswana had been hit with an event like this only once in the last century. A low-pressure system had trapped two converging fronts, stalling the massive storm above their heads. It had been raining heavily now for more than three hours and it showed no signs of stopping. According to the forecast, the rain could last up to thirty-six hours.

As the others discussed the intricacies of how warming polar regions had slowed the mechanisms driving these storms, Kea found her mind drifting. Someone mentioned Houston, then someone argued that event had been coastal. If a storm of this magnitude was happening here, then major change could have untold consequences on the biosphere.

R.J. Corgan

Kea hadn't stayed to hear the rest. Something had been bothering her. Perhaps it was simply that the faculty didn't appear to be taking any time to mourn Tristan's death. Positing scientific theories were their way of dealing with things, but it wasn't hers.

As soon as she could, Kea had fled to the seclusion of her shower.

Now, watching the water gurgle as it slipped into the darkness of the drain, Gwen's words echoed in her head. If the rain stopped, it would be possible to evacuate the camp in a few hours, but given the conditions of the roads, it would likely be days before they could get out.

Days.

Kea groaned.

Trapped with a killer.

Again.

She raised her head to the heavens and felt the jets of water sting her cheeks. "What the hell did I ever do to piss you off?"

***

Kea assembled her research station: bed, tea, platypus, laptop, and complimentary super fluffy bathrobe. *Check. Check. Check. Check. Check.*

She had figured out why the attitude of the others bothered her. It wasn't just that they weren't grieving or that they wanted to focus all their energies on leaving that irritated her. It was that she couldn't face their acceptance of what the poachers had done, of what might have happened to Tristan. Having conveyed their plight to the wardens by satellite phone, they seemed content to wait for help to arrive, even if it meant waiting out the storm with a killer.

She booted up her laptop and followed the instructions Mani had given her to use the 'emergency only' satellite connection.

He can bill me.

She flipped through the last set of images taken by the colony cameras, enjoying the sense of purpose that filled her. Energy drinks notwithstanding, she felt alive. She had formulated a plan. Well, a partial plan, or at least a close approximation of one. After weighing all the options, and possibly against all odds, she had decided to trust people. Well, one person.

Albeit grudgingly.

After all, her therapist had told her she needed to grow as a person and interact more with other people. He had probably meant joining a jazzercise class, however, not attempting to solve a homicide. She shrugged. *Everyone needs a hobby.*

Digging through the files, she couldn't find much footage of the attack itself. The poachers appeared to have smashed the cameras from behind, so there was no documentation of what they'd done to the poor creatures and, hopefully, no traumatized children viewers. However, there was one instance where the camera spun around as it fell. Most of the frames were blurred, but one or two captured one of the men responsible.

Kea studied his receding hairline, high cheekbones, and mud-caked khakis. His eyebrows were wild and untamed, like two drunk caterpillars had taken up ultimate fighting, but he was otherwise unremarkable, except for the fact that he was Asian and that the hair in his nostrils were in desperate need of trimming. She took a couple of screen captures, renamed their files with the date and times, and dropped them into a folder to give to the authorities, whenever they showed up.

Otherwise unremarkable...

She pulled Platy close and stroked the tuft of hair on the toy's head, lost in thought. *Except I've seen you before...somewhere.*

It took her another hour to dig through the footage before she found him. When she had first reviewed the camp's footage, she had been searching for whoever might have put the spider in Addi's cabin. Her attention had been focused on just that, Addi's cabin. That's it. Anything else that had taken place around Mack Camp, she had just skimmed, trying not to drown in the sheer volume of data.

Now, looking at footage from other cameras around the camp, she made a few discoveries. The first was less of a revelation but at least explained why she had so much trouble falling asleep that first night.

"So that's what you've been up to," she muttered as she watched Tshepo slip between the cabins.

The second discovery meant that she was going to have to have a long chat with Tamaya, one she was not looking forward to in the least. It was the third discovery that made her punch the air in triumph.

"Got you!" she exclaimed.

"I missed you too," her computer replied.

Kea froze. "I'm...sorry?" she stammered.

"It's been more than a year," the voice was feminine, exotic, and silky. Authoritative, yet kind.

I know that voice.

Confident that her laptop had not attained sentience, Kea tabbed through her applications and discovered that her webchat software was running. She tapped the screen and brought up the application window. A woman's face appeared, framed with curls of graying hair, gold earrings, and riotously fabulous scarf.

It was Amirah, the woman who had saved her life in Iceland. *Mind you,* Kea thought, *it was partly Amirah's fault my life had needed saving in the first place.*

"Amirah," Kea began suspiciously. "How did you do that? I didn't have the microphone running, let alone the chat application." *Or the camera.*

Very slowly, she tucked Platy out of sight behind her.

"Working for my new employer has certain...advantages." Amirah smiled. "Although *I* don't get to go on luxury safaris."

"It's not a safari...hang on," Kea's eyes darted around the tent, as if looking for other cameras. "How do you know where I am? Are you tracking my IP?"

Amirah laughed. "Not right now, no. There's no need. You keep showing up on one of the world's most popular live streaming documentaries."

While the explanation made sense, Kea still felt as if she were being stalked. "While's it's great to hear from you, it's a bit creepy how you're doing this. What's this about?"

"As I said, there are certain benefits working for my new employer, and I couldn't help thinking about your situation." Amirah waggled her fingers at the screen as if deep in thought, but no doubt she just did it to show off the golden cartouches painted on her long purple nails. "How difficult it is to examine the natural world over the long-term, you said, with cuts in funding and changing faculty."

For a moment, Kea thought Amirah was referring to Addi, then realized the woman was referring to the Icelandic expedition. Kea tried to dial down her paranoia a bit and listen to the woman's proposal. Ten minutes later, she disconnected the call, found a bandage and taped it over the laptop's camera lens, then uninstalled the chat program.

She checked her e-mail, looking for one of the facility messages that she had ignored in all the chaos. There it was, the science building at her university had been broken into at night. As she remembered, nothing had been stolen. She checked the date. It was the same day she showed up at Mack Camp. Her first debut on camera. *Coincidence? Or perhaps Amirah wasn't the only one following her exploits online.*

She turned to address Platy, still wedged underneath the pillow. "I'm going to do something about this. I don't know what and I don't know how, but I'll figure out something. Otherwise, I'm never going to get any sleep ever again. This has to end."

Right now, however, she had other fish to fry.

***

Kea ducked into Carter's cabin, folding the flap closed behind her to keep out the rain that continued to drench the camp. "I really need to talk to Tamaya, but before I do…"

An explosion of pillows, underthings, and a lamp flew up from the sofa.

"Oh my God!" Kea gasped, her jaw agape.

Carter fell on the floor and scrambled to cover his crotch with a pillow. Above him, two bare legs and a naked torso lingered in mid-slide over the edge of the couch. It dangled there for a long, ponderous moment, followed by a crash as the body completed its tumble. Another crash echoed as a flailing leg smashed into another lamp.

Kea stared at the grand piano in the corner, incredulous. "That's a Steinway! In a desert! What is with this place?"

"Can I help you?" Carter gasped.

"What? Oh, sorry." Kea turned her attention back to him. "I wanted to talk to you about using your lab." She heard another thump from behind the sofa. "How about I just wait for you there?"

***

Twenty minutes later, Carter joined her beside the laboratory trailer.

"Look," she began, but Carter waved her silent.

"I don't want to hear it," Carter said quietly as he unlocked the trailer. "No one can find out about us. Botswana is not San Diego."

"I know." Kea had seen Tshepo enter Carter's tent on the recordings and, although she wanted to forget the memories, she'd personally heard the ensuing antics her first night here. Their relationship also explained the look of horror when Tshepo saw Carter had fallen into the water. "And I don't care. At all."

Which was true, although there was something on the recordings that she did want to talk to Tshepo about, but that would have to wait. For now, she wanted to test a hunch. In order to do that, she needed a lab and a forensic scientist. Out here, Carter was as close as she was going to get.

"I need your help." She tapped to Tristan's Camelback that she held nestled in a towel. "I'm going to give it to the authorities when they get here." She followed him into the trailer. "But in the meantime, I want to test a theory."

As she outlined what she wanted to do, he appeared distracted, annoyed. No doubt he was more concerned that Kea would out his activities to Tshepo's wife or family. Still, he was curious enough to slip on a pair of latex gloves and extract the transparent bladder. She watched over his shoulder as he inspected the nozzle of the hose. She hadn't been able to detect anything out of the ordinary, aside from the terrible smell of watermelon.

'Tristan's the only one who touches that stuff.' The memory tingled in her head. *Who had said that? Tamaya? Gwen?*

Carter held the bladder up to a lamp and stared at the flavor crystals that had collected at the base. A shade of yellow-white, the particles looked like grains of neon colored sugar. *Not completely unlike the texture of rat poison crystals.*

"If what killed Tristan was from something he drank, and not something he ate," she theorized, "the last thing he drank was from here."

"And not the first thing?" Carter asked. "Was he drinking out of it all day, or only after lunch?"

"We all had coffee in the morning," she remembered. "Although I wasn't with him the whole day. Since it was raining, it's possible he didn't drink any water 'til later. I know I didn't."

Of course, she thought, *if it had been something he ate, or if something had bitten him, she had no way to prove those scenarios. Not until they found the body.* She stared at the plastic bladder. The contents could be deadly or just vile. They had to know for sure.

"Why come to me?" Carter's tone implied that he knew why she was asking, but he was forcing her to say it out loud.

Kea waited a long moment before finally admitting, "We need to know if it's poison or not."

"You mean we need someone to test it on."

"Unless you have another idea." Morally, she couldn't bring herself to test it on a living creature, but since he was a biologist, among other things, she could live with him doing it, assuming the animal was small enough and preferably non-furry. She looked pointedly at his terrarium.

"You want to poison my frogs." To give him credit, he sounded legitimately offended. "You want to poison Beatrice."

"Well..." she trailed off. *I don't want to. I want you to do it.* For some reason, it seemed too horrible to say.

It was the only reason she had asked him rather than performing the experiment on her own. On the one hand, she was glad she had asked, rather than commit frog-icide behind his back. On the other hand, now she felt even worse for insisting.

"I didn't know you named them..." she said lamely. "I did some research," she continued, hoping he'd hop on board with her plan. "There are plenty of articles on different poisons used on rodents." She shuddered, trying to rinse the experience out of her memories.

"Some take several days or weeks to kill," she said, "which isn't the case here. I'm working on the assumption that this toxin acted quite quickly, which narrows down the possibilities. If we immerse the frogs in samples with water from the camelback..."

"The frogs' skin will quickly absorb it and they'll die." Carter finished for her, shaking his head. "That's repugnant."

"And if the poison was in the watermelon powder," she pressed, "we can test it. I took all of it out of the main hall. Actually, after I read about the disturbing effects of cyanide and something called 1080, a particularly nasty poison one, I removed all the flavor crystals, just to be safe." She waved outside the trailer where she had stacked the canisters. "We should test all of them."

R.J. Corgan

"Cyanide was used at Nikita's colony," Carter confirmed. "But they may have used another airborne spray as well." His shoulders sagged as he seemed to give in to her logic. "Let's spare the frogs, but I still have the tadpoles."

Kea winced. It seemed somehow worse to use babies, but since these were his specimens, she kept her mouth shut.

Using a miniature net, he scooped some of the tadpoles out of the tank and reluctantly plopped them one by one into little plastic cups.

"Sorry guys," Kea muttered as she pulled on a pair of gloves. "I hope I'm wrong."

In the first cup she added tap water and the watermelon crystals from the faculty table in the main hall. After a few minutes of swimming in the cloudy water, the tadpole appeared to be behaving normally. Carter cautioned that, depending on the poison, it might not have any effect on the tadpole's metabolism. They moved on to the next cup, this one with water and strawberry powder. They repeated the process for all the other flavors.

Nothing happened.

So far for good. All tadpoles appeared to be swimming...swimmingly. *At least we aren't dealing with a mass poisoner.*

In the last cup, Carter poured out a portion of the watermelon flavored water from Tristan's bladder. He swirled it around to ensure it was properly mixed. Kea would have tested the bladder water first, but she suspected Carter was reluctant to harm his specimen and waited until the last possible moment. She heard him whisper an apology as he placed a tadpole into the cup.

The response was immediate.

The tadpole twitched and jerked in agony.

"Sorry buddy," Carter slumped onto the stool and watched as it died.

Kea stared at the remaining tadpoles that swam around in their water-flavored prisons. They were safe at least, and possibly enjoying their new-found sugar highs.

"Let me get this straight." Judging from his tone, Carter appeared to finally be taking her seriously. "You think someone mixed poison in the watermelon crystals on the faculty table?"

Kea nodded. "Either at night or in the morning before we left to take down the sites. At some point between then and now, they replaced it with regular powder. I suppose that it's possible that someone snuck it into his flask during the fieldwork, but that would mean that the killer was either you, me, or Tshepo, and I imagine that if it was one of us, we'd be smart enough not to let him drive."

"Unless it's a double bluff." Carter regarded her suspiciously, no doubt in the same manner that she was eying him.

"It's possible," she agreed. She was going on gut instinct by trusting Carter. He seemed to have the least connection to Addi or Tristan, and nothing to gain by their deaths.

The fact that someone could even take the risk of poisoning so many people horrified her, and she wondered if it was even the plan at all. *Was done in the spur of the moment?*

Carter blew out a breath. "So that leaves, who? Mani, Katherine, Gwen and…Tamaya?"

"In theory." She hated guessing. They needed more data. "But it has to be someone who had access to the poison at Boudicca's colony."

"Tshepo wasn't in the field. Gwen never got near the stuff, she worked the gambits." He ticked off names on his fingers. "Only Mani and Katherine collected the field samples. And me, of course. Although Tamaya insisted on examining the bodies and the poison when she got back from the hospital that night."

Which really means only Mani or Katherine, Kea thought. *Tamaya would never do something like this.*

Why did all the facts keep pointing back to Tamaya?

"It isn't just access to the poison," Kea reasoned. "It would have to be someone with access to the main hall. Before the morning shift, presumably…"

"That probably won't narrow it down much…" Carter said grimly. "We all go in and out of the main hall. Anyone could have swapped it out, either in the morning or at night."

"The cameras might help narrow it down," she suggested. "I'll have another look to see if there is any footage of the main hall last night."

Carter scooped the living tadpoles from their cups with a net. He gently rinsed them off before returning them to their tank. "Okay. I gotta place a call to the wardens and tell them about this."

"There's something I want to ask you first. It's about Tshepo." She averted her eyes as she explained about the poacher she had seen on the camera. "The thing is, I looked back at the feeds for last week and saw the same man talking to Tshepo outside his cabin."

Carter looked blankly at her. Then, as realization slowly dawned, his expression darkened. "You think Tshepo's connected to the poachers?"

She shrugged. "I find it odd that when the poachers got here, not only were most of the staff and guards gone, but the poachers didn't take anything other than the ATVs."

Carter raised his fist as if to hit the table, then changed the movement, using his thumb to rub his brow instead. His movements were stiff and jerky, as if he was physically processing his anger. "Why?"

"Maybe it's for the money, maybe they have leverage over him…" She didn't need to spell out the implications of their nightly trysts.

"No," Carter said vehemently. "I mean what's the point of killing Tristan? Or Addi? Who would want to kill both of them?"

Kea bit her lip. "If I knew that…I wouldn't have had to ask for your help."

"It just doesn't fit." Carter seemed to still be trying to take all the new information in. "As a paramedic, you see people get killed all the time. Outside of accidents, if someone is killed, it's usually the result of a domestic dispute or drunken brawls. It's quick. It's blind rage. I don't think I ever saw a real murder on shift. At least not one that someone planned out. There's usually too much time to rationalize the penalties, the complications, to change your mind."

Kea, who had once been hunted for sport, declined to comment. Instead, she asked, "Which do you think happened to Addi and Tristan? Rash or planned?"

"Both," Carter concluded. "The poison was sloppy and high risk. Too many other people could have been hurt. The spider, though, that would take forethought."

"Well, we've got the 'how' part worked out," Kea said. "Now the tricky part is to figure out who did it."

"You sound awfully eager."

She shrugged. "I may have done this once before."

"You caught a murderer?" Carter asked in disbelief.

"Well, not exactly," Kea squirmed. "I first accused the wrong person by mistake. Then I got pushed down a crevasse by the real killer and was left for dead."

He looked at her in astonishment.

"Practice makes perfect, right?" She patted Carter on the shoulder as she made for the trailer door. "Why don't you have a word with Tshepo, then we call the authorities?"

She left before he could change his mind. It was still possible that he could be the killer. He certainly had the medical background to have committed both crimes. However, he had seemed genuinely traumatized by the death of a tadpole, so she wasn't sure he had it in him to kill anyone. Plus, he seemed very put out by the notion that Tshepo might have had something to do with the poachers.

Kea's thoughts kept returning to the empty mug that she had used to smash the hair band this morning. It hadn't been there when she fell asleep. Which meant that Tamaya had been in the kitchen before coming to bed.

She remembered what she had told Gwen about the locked room...tent mystery surrounding Addi. No one else had gone in or out. No one except Tamaya. If Tamaya had been in the kitchen and had access to the poison, she was the only possible suspect with means and opportunity for both deaths.

Assuming, of course, there was only one killer.

She was halfway to Tamaya's cabin when she realized that she forgot to ask which frog was Beatrice.

***

Tamaya was sitting cross-legged on her bed. Her computer screen was filled with a scientific article, still apparently in mid-draft. From the look on Tamaya's tear-stained face, Kea doubted she was getting any editing done.

The awkward, oblong shape of the satellite phone filled Kea's hand. She tapped it against her leg nervously, unable to contain her pent-up energy. *Decisions, decisions.*

R.J. Corgan

"We need to talk," Kea said at last.

Tamaya kept her eyes on the screen.

Kea found herself wavering, uncertain how to handle this. Eventually, she found the strength to ask, "Were you in the kitchen last night?"

Tamaya nodded. "I always get hot chocolate around midnight. Helps me sleep. Everyone knows that."

"Oh, Tamaya…" Kea slumped onto the bed beside her and explained about the poisoned drink powder. "They're going to be checking the tapes of anyone who had access to both the poison and the powder." She paused, hating herself for having to add, "Worse, you're the only person who had the opportunity to kill both Tristan and Addi."

Tamaya bristled, quivering with rage. "Kea, that's insane…"

"I know." She held up the phone. "That's why I wanted to talk to you before I told the authorities. There's no way you would have poisoned Tristan, let alone put everyone else at risk. Aside from the fact that I know you're not capable of it, there's no motive. And I would never believe that you'd hurt Addi."

Tamaya shifted uncomfortably on the bed. "I didn't kill Tristan, I swear. And I didn't kill Addi, believe me," she implored. "No one killed Addi. It was an accident. A terrible, goddamn accident." She gasped for air, as if forgetting how to breathe. Whatever righteous anger she had been holding back flooded out of her.

Reflexively, Kea hugged her tight. "I know. I know. We'll get this sorted out. It'll be okay. We'll figure it out." She pulled back and looked her friend directly in the eyes. "But you have to be completely honest with me. I know there's something you're not telling me. What is it?"

Kea thought that she saw something tremble inside Tamaya, then break. "It's all going to look even worse, you know. So much worse." Tamaya sniffed, using her t-shirt to wipe her nose. "Addi and Tristan just patented one of their machine learning algorithms. They'd partnered with a couple of the big internet giants."

"Wait a sec," Kea said slowly. "Are you telling me they were rich?"

"Not yet." Tamaya shook her head. "It's the royalties. Once the system goes live, then they'd start collecting."

132

"And now that..." Kea groped for the best way to phrase it. "Now that they're not around anymore?"

Tamaya sank backward onto the bed and stared up at the ceiling. "It all goes to me."

"All? Why?"

"With Addi dead, his shares go to me." Tamaya sniffed again. Her nose was a mess, but at least her breathing had steadied. "Addi was terrible with business. I think he brought me on to keep an eye on Tristan. Now that Tristan's gone, according to the succession plan, I have full control of the company."

"Tamaya," Kea said gravely. "You know what this means."

Her friend was already tied to both deaths, and now the word 'motive' might as well be scrawled across the sky for everyone to see. "This does not look good."

Tamaya didn't answer. Instead, she lay on the bed, barely breathing.

"Okay," Kea said after a beat. "Stay here and keep the door...I mean, keep the tent flap, closed. Right now, no one knows how Tristan died, so if there is a killer out there, they're not likely to make a move. Not if they think they got away with it."

Assuming, of course, the killer wasn't Carter or Tshepo. Or both. *Or...Who else was there? Katherine, Gwen, and...*

"What are you going to do?" Tamaya asked listlessly.

Something clicked in Kea's memory. She wasn't certain, however, and she'd have to double check the records in her tent. "I have to see a man about a Pumpkin King."

Chapter 10 – Prison Walls Are Never Built to Scale

KEA SAT atop a hilltop and observed the hustle and bustle of the camp. Packs of students heaved in and out of the main hall. The meerkats were winding down for the evening. The sentinels kept watch as the rest lazily groomed each other and herded the pups safely inside the tunnels. The lenses of the video cameras glittered in the rays of the setting sun.

It all looks so peaceful. Pity it isn't real.

The weight of Gwen's AV glasses made her nose itch. Inside the shelter of her tent, she could hear the rain pouring outside. She wiggled her bum on her bed to ease out a kink in her lower back. Raising her gloved hands, she compressed them together in a rapid gesture. The recorded view of the colony shrank, reducing it to a fraction of its scale. At this resolution, the animated people and meerkats automatically turned off, but the entire campground was visible, trapped inside the day it had been captured by the drone.

It was all so small, she thought, *so fragile.*

Using the gloves, she was able to drop a virtual point on the map. She could use the voice control to populate little text balloons and anchor them to the locations. For practice, she labeled the main hall. Then, looking west, she dropped a point and a balloon on Tamaya and Addis' cabin. Then she added *'Death by spider'* inside the same bubble.

Where had everyone else been that night?

She labeled all the cabins: Mani, Gwen, Katherine, and Carter. She added Tshepo to Carter's balloon. As far as crime maps went, she considered, it was a little lacking.

What was the connection between Tristan and Addi's deaths?

She zoomed out and pawed at the air to move the landscape beneath her. She traced the road as it wound through the hills before it was swallowed by the sands and brush. Finding the wash where they nearly died in the flood, she dropped more points, one for the jeep, one for Tristan, and one for each person: herself, Tshepo, and Carter. She made a big red one for 'Rhinos/Poachers.' She panned over to the poisoned meerkat colonies and dropped more points labeled 'Poison.'

Would the poachers want Tristan dead? Would they want Addi dead? To remove the expedition completely?

Addi perhaps, she considered, but she doubted they even knew who Tristan was. The specific way he'd been poisoned suggested intimate knowledge of his habits. Everyone who had contact with the poison might have been able to kill Tristan, or even, at a stretch, Addi. While the doors had been covered by the cameras, anyone could have slipped into Addi's tent from behind. *Who would want both of them dead?*

Aside from Mani of course. He acted like everything was fine, but that was what he would want everyone to think, if he was going to start murdering people.

Kea took off the AV glasses and mulled over the options. It wasn't Gwen who had pointed out that Tristan was the only one who used the watermelon powder. *'Only Skellington drinks that stuff.'* Kea hadn't understood the reference at the time, but once it clicked, she had pulled up the files to learn who else was on Mani's panel. No surprise, Tristan was the second person on the list.

She knew first-hand the hostility that could enter the teacher-student relationship. Indeed, she had seen too many headlines of university professors who had been murdered by their frustrated graduate students. Mani's permanent scowl and imposing figure hovered over her thoughts. *He was definitely not someone to cross*, she thought.

However, she couldn't imagine why he waited until now to knock them off, unless this trip provided the opportunity for convenient accidents. Or, perhaps, he had waited until he could figure out a way to frame someone else, like Tamaya.

If it was Mani, she reasoned, there was one more person on his defense panel. One more person to kill.

She flipped through her notes. Usually the third person on the panel would be an external from another university, but the files noted that an exception had been made. She flinched when she re-read the name. *Of course, it would be Katherine.*

The thought that the woman might be in danger spurred Kea to put on her boots and head across camp once more.

***

R.J. Corgan

The rain was still pouring. The droplets slipped off the brim of Kea's hood in irregular sputters, as if the sky itself was drooling on her. As she stomped along the muddy trail that marked the camp's outer perimeter, she found she didn't mind. At least she was outside. She had spent too many hours cooped up, wondering who had done what to whom. It was beyond depressing.

Letting her feet mindlessly stomp down the path, she considered her options. This trip ultimately, was a delay. The deaths, the murders, the meerkats, all of this was just putting off the inevitable. Eventually, after the storm, after the funeral, she would have to go home and decide what she was going to do with her life. Living out of her office, relying on sleeping pills to get through each night, and doing research that she no longer found interesting, was not healthy.

Assuming, of course, she wasn't murdered first.

"I remember a time when I didn't have thoughts like these," she whispered to a spikey lump of agave. "Just ones about 'what am I not going to cook for dinner?'"

The plant merely dripped with water, as if politely waiting for her to pass.

The baobab tree, when she reached it, was slightly more accommodating, parting the cascading sheets of rain and offering some slender shadows of comfort. She stood underneath it and took a long breath of the cool air.

She was soaking wet, drenched in rainfall. In Africa. In the frigging Kalahari.

And someone is trying to kill people, a little part of her mind reminded her.

Fine.

She had to find Mani before he found Katherine. The lights in both of their cabins had been off, so she had walked the perimeter to see where else they might be. The equipment shed and the main hall were both illuminated, as was the pool, which was unexpected.

Deciding she needed to arm herself before any confrontation, she headed for the kitchen to swipe a knife. Exiting via the main hall she discovered that the rest of the camp staff were waiting out the storm by playing board games. Gwen sat away from the group, perched on a bench, her hands clicking away with her knitting needles. Sock rested in her lap and a glass of wine was nestled within skeins of yarn on a bench beside her.

"When I have to wait something out, I try to use the time to challenge myself to try a new technique," Gwen explained. She held up Sock, who now looked vaguely British. "This stitch is my new favorite. It's called *Gingham Style*."

Kea suppressed a groan, made some hasty excuses, and retreated to the relative safety of the pool.

When the students had infested the camp, she had avoided this place, reluctant to mingle in her bathing suit. It amazed her how much water this place splashed around in a desert, even though Tamaya had informed her that it was constructed on a natural spring. *It still smacked of excess, though.*

In the pattering rain, the pool appeared particularly redundant. The storm had coated the surface with fronds and litter, fouling the blue waters. The chairs had been folded up by the staff into a single line and tied down. A figure sat in one of the remaining sun chairs under one of the eves that lined the bar, sipping out of a large flagon.

Carter.

She leant on the bar and inspected the large metal jug in his hands. It had the image of a dragon emblazoned on its side. "The pellet with the poison's in the vessel with the pestle, the flagon with the dragon has the brew that is true," she murmured. "Where on earth did you get that thing?"

Carter grunted.

"What, no grand story? No, 'Angela Lansbury and I used to hike the Appalachian Trail?'" Kea teased. Receiving no response, she took in his steely face and his sorrow filled eyes. "What did Tshepo have to say?"

He took a long drink, then clutched the jug against his chest, as if he were cradling an infant. "Would you believe," he said and waved a hand around as if to encompass the pool, the bar, and the rest of the camp, "that this place is deeply in debt?"

"I'm shocked. Shockingly shocked. Ben-Franklin-with-a-kite-in-a-storm shocked-"

Carter shushed her. "Tshepo got a loan from China to renovate this place and now he's in a hole he can't get out of. Occasionally, that man you saw on the camera, comes through with his men, and

R.J. Corgan

Tshepo looks the other way." He gazed into the opening of the flagon and sloshed the contents around. "Usually, they only take one or two tusks, but lately they've been a bit greedier."

"And the cameras? The meerkats? Why did they do that?"

"They didn't exactly provide Tshepo with a PowerPoint briefing of their plans." Carter took another long drink. "He thinks they're not thrilled about the public exposure this place gets with Addi's team here."

"Are you going to turn him in?"

Carter's fingers drummed a staccato rhythm against the flagon's belly. "They aren't just holding the money over him. They have pictures, of us together." He sighed and stared up at the night sky. "I've only known the guy for two weeks, and I've helped destroy his life."

Did they also try to force Addi to close the expedition? Kea wondered. She felt her mind reel again. *One thing at time.*

She pushed off from the bar and offered him her hand. "Wanna help me save someone else's life?"

He looked up at her curiously.

"Bring the flagon," she added. "We may need it for thumping."

***

The equipment store was the largest building in the camp, hidden from view among the colonial style luxurious tents. Kea and Carter threaded their way toward it, crouching as they snuck through the lines of the remaining recreational quad bikes that tourists used to off-road through the deserts in the dry winter months. The skeleton of an ancient yellow Chevette hunkered near the hut, dark and lonely, as if brooding.

"You actually think Mani's trying to kill everyone on his panel?" Carter whispered in disbelief.

Kea motioned for him to be quiet and ushered him behind the husk of an abandoned generator.

"He knew that only Tristan drank the watermelon powder." She kept her voice low as she scouted the surroundings.

"So what? We all know that."

Kea felt her stomach clench. "Now you tell me this?" she hissed in disbelief. "Why didn't you mention that when we found the poison?"

A loud clank echoed from the front of the building, as if a wrench had fallen to the floor.

"Even if he is killing everyone who was on his panel," Carter pressed, "what are you going to do about it?"

She tapped the pocket of her jacket where she'd hidden her phone. "Record his statement then get the hell out of there."

"That's insane. The man kickboxes for fun." Carter bent down and picked up the rusted remains of an old crowbar.

She winced. "I'll be quick then. Just be ready to shut him inside. After I get out."

A cry came from inside the building.

Katherine.

Kea braced herself to run, reaching for the blade tucked into the back of her waistband.

Carter held her back. "I don't think that's a cry for help."

The cry continued before trailing off into something completely different.

More of a moan.

Oh, for God's sake. Am I the only one not having sex? Another thought struck her. *Katherine was on his panel.* The audacity of it floored her. *And he still didn't pass.*

Kea hunched down behind the generator again and tried to reboot her brain. If Mani wasn't trying to kill everyone on his panel and everyone knew about the powder...*Who could it not be?*

She mentally went through the facts again. Gwen didn't have access to the poison. She was placing her bets that it wasn't Tshepo, Carter, or Tamaya. *Please don't let it be Tamaya.*

That only left one possible suspect.

There was a crescendo of cries from the equipment store, then silence.

Finding it difficult to focus, Kea shook her head clear of the mental image of Katherine and Mani together. Unbidden, it was replaced by the memory of Tshepo and Carter. *Not helpful.*

The silence from inside the building was replaced with the sounds of the shifting of tools and the *tink* of belt buckles.

Kea could imagine Katherine as a killer. In fact, the woman was probably the type to diagram a murder ahead of time with charts, whiteboards, and figurines.

Kea risked a peek around the debris and glimpsed Mani slipping out of the building. She vacillated between following him or going straight to Katherine. *What motive could the woman possibly have to kill?*

In a flash, a comment Katherine had made came back to her. It had been at the last dinner, regarding the matriarch meerkat's perchance for killing the offspring of others. *'A mother will do anything to ensure the survival of their children.'*

Kea sprinted lightly across the muddy terrain to the entrance of the doorway, dragging Carter with her. "Wait here." Ignoring his frantic motions to stay put, she stepped into the building, hoping that she'd given Katherine enough time to make herself decent.

"I don't think I'm ready yet for another round...oh, it's you." Katherine was in the middle of lacing up her boots when Kea approached. "Everything alright?"

"I hope so." Out of breath, Kea scanned the room for anyone else who might be lurking inside. The facility was dark and shadowy, a stark contrast to the rest of the resort. Grime and sand seemed to have nestled their way into every corner and the cement floor was scarred with pools of oil. The windows had been sealed against the storm from the outside.

This just might work.

"I wanted to have a word." Kea related what she knew about Tristan's death and the poisoned powder. As she talked, she was careful to position herself between Katherine and the exit.

"The flavor crystals? Seriously?" Katherine returned to lacing her boot, seemingly more annoyed than worried. "Well, we'll need to have his body and that powder examined properly. I can't imagine why anyone would want him dead, he was so...ineffectual."

"That's what I'm trying to figure out." Kea folded her arms across her chest. "Before someone else dies."

Katherine seemed to finally realize what Kea was implying.

"I don't kill people," Katherine said wearily. "People don't kill people out here, at least not over meerkats. This is probably just an accident, like the spider."

Kea let silence speak for itself.

"Oh, I see. You still think I killed Addi?" Katherine pulled a scrunchie out of her pocket and gathered her hair up into a tight bun.

"Look, we need to get everyone together and wait for help. We don't have time for you to play Nancy Drew. Besides aren't you a bit old for the part?"

Letting the jibe pass, Kea talked out her theory. "After all these years, you're still in the trenches," she posited. "While old Addi lorded over all as the department chair."

"Kea, I hate to break it to you, but I'm not going to kill my ex-husband over a promotion. Lord knows I'd have enough other reasons over the years to have tried to kill him before now," Katherine conceded. "But murder has a way of stopping alimony checks. Now, we've discussed this before, so I'm done with it." She cast about the shelving by the desk lifting papers and shifting boxes. "Now, where the hell did I put my phone…"

Kea continued, annoyed at Katherine's apparent disregard. "I couldn't quite figure out how you did it…"

"I didn't do anything," Katherine cut in. "I wasn't anywhere near Addi the night he died. I was with Mani that night…"

Kea stopped her, not wanting more visuals. "I couldn't work out the connection between the two deaths, but then I remembered something Tristan said about p-hacking."

"P-hacking?" Katherine was clearly exasperated now, although possibly more about not being able to find her phone than having to talk to Kea.

"It's about looking at data with the intent of finding a pattern, of trying to connect two different things when they aren't there." Kea spoke carefully, watching to see Katherine's reaction. "I couldn't see the connection."

Katherine, having abandoned her search, faced Kea, her arms folded across her chest.

"Until I realized there wasn't any," Kea concluded. "You didn't kill Addi. You couldn't have, no one could have. And that's when it all fell into place."

Okay, so until five minutes ago, I thought it was Mani, but still…

Katherine threw her hands up in the air. "Okay, so how am I supposed to have done whatever this is. Just tell me so we can get on with securing the camp."

"I think Addi's death was an accident after all," Kea admitted. "But when you learned he was dead and then that cyanide fell into

R.J. Corgan

your lap, you realized how easy it would be to take out Tristan and pin the blame for both deaths on Tamaya. It was just too good to resist." She shifted slightly, hoping that the phone was still recording every word, although she was worried the pose looked a little obvious.

"With Addi gone," Kea continued, "Tamaya still stood between you and Addi's share of the money. You needed to get her out of the way."

"I don't know how many times I have to tell you this," Katherine seethed, "so I'll say it very slowly this time: I. Do. Not. Get. Any. Of. Addi's. Money."

"You don't," Kea agreed. "But Rocco does. And a mother would do anything for their child, wouldn't they? Getting the job of department chair would just be the cherry on top."

Katherine frowned, as if considering for the first time how this situation might look to the authorities. "And how, exactly, are you going to prove that I'm a cyanide wielding, black ex-widow poisoner?"

Kea had been afraid she might ask that question. She couldn't prove that Katherine had administered the poison. She didn't have so much as a single fingerprint's worth of evidence and Katherine hadn't admitted to anything.

Kea took a step backward, feeling the doorframe pressing against her back. As if sensing her sudden discomfort, Katherine cocked her head. She looked drained then, not afraid, not scared, just tired.

"I'll be sure to pass on your suspicions to my lawyer, once I get one." Katherine stepped away from the workbench, moving toward Kea and the door.

It was then that Kea spied the bodies of the other meerdroids on the bench behind Katherine, their innards splayed out across the surface. And something clicked.

"You know," Kea began, "after Addi was bitten, I searched the entire server for any video files and I never found one that matched the view from your functioning meerdroid in Genevieve's colony."

Katherine paused.

Kea pressed once more. "Either they were never loaded onto the server in the first place or someone deleted them...If I remember from its position, that camera would have been facing the medical store."

142

Judging from the stricken expression on Katherine's face, Kea knew she'd hit a home run.

"What are you hiding? What was on those files?"

Katherine stood completely still. "Leave it, Kea. Just walk away."

"Now that sounds like the most sensible thing anyone's said since I got here," Kea said sweetly. "But I also think we'd all feel a lot better if we could keep an eye on you." With that, she slipped out of the door and slammed it shut. Carter helped slip the crowbar through the handle. She found the sound of Katherine's furious pounding on the door immensely satisfying.

"Now what?" Carter asked.

Kea shrugged. "We wait."

"You locked her in the equipment shed," Carter protested.

"We're surrounded by tents," Kea replied, annoyed that she seemed to be the one who had to think of everything. "It's the *only* building we can lock her in."

"Yes, but we've locked her in the equipment shed," Carter repeated. "With all the *equipment.*"

As if on cue, they heard the whine of the electric buzz saw.

"I'll just shut off the generators then, shall I?" Carter said wearily, before trudging round to the back of the building.

***

Kea moved along the path to the main hall to get reinforcements. As she walked, she scanned dark voids between the cabins warily. If she was right, Katherine was out of the game for now. If she was wrong or if Katherine hadn't been acting alone, another player might make their move, maybe even Mani. It had happened before. Kea wasn't going to play the fool a second time.

She was just passing her own cabin when she heard an unusual rustling sound. Startled, she paused, peering through the rain to see if she had been followed. It took nearly a minute for the sound to repeat, almost invisible against the white noise of the rain.

There it was again. Her eyes first traced the silhouette of her cabin, then the porch, before alighting on the little shelter she had built for Hazel.

Two beady eyes stared back. No, not two. Eight.

Kea approached slowly. She held out her hand, pretending she had a chunk of egg. Hazel stuck her head out, sniffing the air suspiciously. Beside her, Kea saw the tiny heads of the pups peer out, eager for a meal.

Kea almost broke down in tears. She wanted to hug them, to squeeze them and cry out in delight, but she didn't want to spook the little creatures. Instead, she said, "Wait right there, I'll be back in a flash with some food." She trotted down the path, intent on sharing the news with Tamaya and then fetching some hard-boiled eggs. And, of course, see if Tshepo could help quarantine the new prisoner. As if to match her mood, it appeared that the rain beginning to ease. *About damn time.*

As she ran, she questioned her decision to lock Katherine up. It was the only possible option, she assured herself. Still, using the poison seemed so hasty. Would Katherine be so sloppy?

Again, she thought, if it wasn't Katherine, the only other person it could be was Tamaya. *It can't be.*

Kea's eyes were drawn to the now desolate meerkat colony. She had been avoiding it, averting her gaze, feeling the shame of being human, knowing what humans were capable of doing. Murdering meerkats.

She remembered the conversation from that night at dinner, of meerkats murdering each other. *We aren't so different from our little friends.*

She stared at the colony once more, thinking of Hazel's exile. To think that Hazel survived, saved the pups, that the rover was the one who saved the day…the possibility of the research publications alone would thrill Tamaya, not to mention the media…

The rover.

Kea groaned.

I wonder if I can get Hallmark to invest in printing "I'm sorry I accused you of Murder" cards…

Epilogue

GWEN SLID behind the wheel of the jeep and turned the key. There was a quiet clicking noise, followed by silence.

"I took out the spark plugs." Kea stepped out from behind the storage bins. "It's not going anywhere."

Technically, that was a lie. Kea had no idea how to remove a spark plug and had only disconnected the battery, but she hoped Gwen wouldn't know that.

Kea hadn't even been able to tell anyone else her theory. She only had enough time to check the video recordings of the gambits from Boudicca's colony. They hadn't been wiped. Perhaps Gwen had just forgotten or hadn't known the video was automatically backed up to the cloud. Kea certainly wouldn't have remembered Boudicca's pups if it hadn't been for seeing Hazel on her porch with her own pups.

Before confronting Gwen, Kea had come to disable the jeeps just in case the woman tried to make a run for it. Hearing her approach, Kea had barely enough time to hide behind a crate.

Gwen wore the look of a frightened animal. Her hands tightened on the steering wheel, knuckles bone white.

"I couldn't work out why you didn't tell us about the pups surviving," Kea said, keeping her eyes fixed on Gwen, determined not to look at the tool counter. "Until I reviewed the footage and saw you found the other cyanide canister in the tunnels and retrieved it using the gambit." She shook her head. "I'd say leaving Boudicca's pups to starve was cruel, but that's nothing compared to what you did to Tristan."

"I don't know what you're talking about." Gwen said dully, as if she couldn't inject genuine emotion into the words.

She's debating her options, Kea thought. *To run? Run where? Where did she think she was going to drive off to? Was she even thinking, or just panicking? Or did she just see that the rain was stopping and tried to make a break for it? Or is she thinking of stabbing me with a knitting needle?*

"Here's what I think," Kea said, stalling for time. The gambit camera on the storage bin was recording their conversation, but that wouldn't be any help if Gwen attacked her. Kea was fairly certain she could take the woman if she came at her, but the frightened, feral look in the woman's eyes was worrisome. "You assumed Tamaya killed Addi, didn't you? After all, no one else could have killed him."

There was a long silence. Gwen remained still, unmoving, before finally saying. "I am not an idiot. I know you're recording this. I can see the power light on the gambit."

Mentally cursing, Kea kept talking, as everything suddenly seemed to fit together. Her words rushed to get out, tumbling over each other in the process. "You and Addi had a thing back in school, didn't you? But he picked Tamaya over you. The restraining order had nothing to do with the toilets, not really. She had what you could never have. Yet you think Tamaya let him die, or worse, that she killed him herself. Either way, you'd never have Addi now. She ruined your life and you couldn't let that stand."

Gwen's hands dropped from the wheel, at that, as if Kea finally hit a weak spot.

Kea pressed on. "You realized she was going to get the house and the money. Your property will still be screwed, so you decided that you had to do something. In the tunnels, you happened on an unopened cyanide capsule. You took it but didn't tell anyone."

Seeing Gwen reach for the door of the jeep, Kea spoke quickly, hoping someone would find them, that someone would come in, that someone would help. *Please let someone come.* "But poisoning Tamaya wasn't good enough, someone would figure it out. You knew Tamaya had access to the poison. You knew she would get her nightly hot chocolate from the kitchen, that it would be recorded on camera. You knew about Tristan and Addi's finances and saw it would make it look like Tamaya was doing it for the money. No one would miss Tristan, everyone wanted to kill him anyway. Justice served. Except for one thing. It was just an accident, Gwen. The spider was just an accident. She didn't kill Addi."

Gwen started to weep. She didn't run. She didn't charge at Kea. She just broke down, and Kea saw her for the person she was, hopelessly in love with someone who had never returned her affections and was now gone forever. Worse, her own life was now in ruins as well.

Kea let her hand fall away from the knife hidden in her belt. She walked over to the door, trying not to let the sound of Gwen's tears into her head.

"Where are you going?" The woman sniffed, as if offended Kea would just leave her.

"I have to let a very angry woman out of the equipment shed." She paused, nodding to the jeep. "You might want to lock the doors. This might get very ugly."

***

Katherine, as Kea's mother would say, was more than a trifle disappointed. Once they let her out of the shed, Katherine unleashed a verbal assault that would have made Tarantino blush. While surprised by the colorful expletives, Kea acceded that the retribution was justified.

She was less forgiving of the length of rebar Katherine threw in her direction. However, considering the stick of iron wound up taking out the windshield of a jeep that Kea was not personally liable for, she considered it a tie. That said, Kea planned on keeping at least fifty feet away from the woman in the future.

Carter mentioned the additional possibility Katherine could press legal charges, but Kea hoped it wouldn't come to that. *Although if I keep up my current track record, I might need a lawyer.*

Tshepo offered to keep an eye on Gwen until the officers arrived on site. Kea tried to relate the new developments to Tamaya but discovered that her friend's cabin was deserted. Panicking, Kea noticed that her pack was gone as well. Not wanting to alert the others, Kea did a quick reconnoiter of the camp, but couldn't find a sign of Tamaya anywhere.

Standing by the pool, Kea stared at her reflection, wondering how much more of this she could reasonably handle sober. Then she remembered the dopey look of horror on Tamaya's face the night Addi died. And the look of shame.

Oh, Tamaya...

***

The view from the hill was startling. The remains of the storm clouds huddled at the edge of the horizon, wadded up like discarded bedsheets. The wet sands glistened in the brilliant sunshine. In a matter of hours, most of the water on the pans would be absorbed by the greedy sands or evaporate back into the sky.

The scene was breathtaking.

"I still prefer glaciers." Kea sat down beside Tamaya on one of the roots. "Where'd you think you were going?"

Tamaya shrugged, as if embarrassed. "How did you know where to find me?"

"Remember that tit you dated sophomore year? Simon, I think?"

"Please don't use his name."

"When you thought he'd knocked you up, you ran."

Tamaya snorted. "I got as far as the Pancake Hut."

"You were much easier to find then," Kea reminisced. "No passport. No car. I hoped you'd be here, before you went Walkabout."

Tamaya rested her head on Kea's shoulder.

"Have you been writing Addi's papers for him?" Kea asked.

There was a pause. "Maybe." Tamaya squirmed. "How'd you know?"

Rather than repeat Katherine's unflattering remarks on Tamaya's work, Kea changed track. "It was you wasn't it?" She remembered Tamaya's pale face as she tottered above Addi's writhing body, the slow roll of emotions rippling across her face. "I thought you were just in shock, but he drugged you."

Tamaya nodded. "The drugs were supposed to be for him. He had this idea he could just overdose and be done with it. I stopped him, but the bugger slipped some in my cocoa. His father had the same medical condition, you know." Tamaya blew out a long shuddering breath. "Addi saw what it did to him, but worse than that, he saw what it did to his mother. She was so worn out from trying to take care of his father that she died very young. I think he thought he could spare me that."

"But if they suspected he overdosed deliberately on any medications, even sleeping pills...they'd autopsy and discover it was a suicide..." Kea prompted.

"No insurance payout," Tamaya said with disgust. "Even if you want to die in the states, the government won't let you. We had always talked about maybe doing it out here. But that last day, when he nearly got that kid killed, I think Addi decided it was time. He didn't tell me of course, nor how he had planned to do it."

"He didn't want you to have to watch, did he?" Kea guessed. "That's why he tried to knock you out."

Tamaya ground her fists into her eyes. "Why did he use the spider? It was so...horrible." She sighed. "I doubt he even knew what he was doing, not really."

"Katherine knew, I think." Kea gently stroked Tamaya's head. "I think she knew what was wrong with Addi and suspected what had happened that night. That's why she deleted the videos from the meerdroid. She was protecting him. And you."

"She never said anything to me, but she knew what happened to his father." Tamaya rubbing her wet nose with the back of her hand. "Addi was in and out so much in the last few weeks, I'm not surprised if she caught on. I'm not sure which was worse, watching his body die in agony or watching his mind quietly fall apart. There were times when he couldn't even recognize me."

"That explains the toilets in your yard, I guess," Kea added knowingly.

"Toilets?" Tamaya asked in surprise. "No, that was me. That was my idea."

"Why?" Kea blurted out. "Why would you be *that* person? The person who puts toilets on lawns. It's crazy."

"If it's crazy to make seven hundred and fifty thousand dollars, then yes, I am."

"How much?"

"That's what the city of El Cajon paid for that other tract of land we had. They were desperate to get rid of us by the end. We made around four hundred thousand dollars in profit."

Stunned, Kea found herself at a loss for words.

They sat together and watched as the pans woke from their wet slumber. They saw the birds reclaim the sky and the springbok awkwardly place their feet in the squelching sands.

"Now everyone's going to think I killed Addi and Tristan for their money." Tamaya pressed her cheek against Kea's shoulder. "Will you visit me in prison?"

Tamaya's tone was irreverent, but Kea felt the tears soaking into her shirt. "That depends if you're going to tell them about Addi." Kea

R.J. Corgan

had been weighing this decision on the walk out here. "Clearly Katherine isn't going to say anything, and neither am I. As far as I'm concerned, he stepped on a spider. I do feel, however, that first I should fill you in what our nifty knitter has been up to. The short version is, you're off the hook. Pardon the pun. Oh, wait, that would be crochet I suppose. I'm rubbish at these." She sighed. "Poor Tristan."

Tamaya sobbed quietly, quaking as she hugged her friend.

"That reminds me," Kea said eventually. "I have some new houseguests back at camp that I think you'll want to see. Plus, we need to get back to Boudicca's camp as soon as possible…"

***

A twitter announced the arrival of Hazel.

"I know, I know." Kea sat down beside the box on the porch of her cabin. "I should be in bed. You should be too."

Hazel twittered again.

Hesitantly, Kea reached out. The meerkat didn't shy away and let Kea stroke her back.

"She trusts you." Carter walked up the path and loitered at the base of the steps.

"Everyone makes mistakes." Kea noted that the pups that Hazel rescued from Genevieve's colony kept to the shadows in the back of the box. She had tossed some egg to them earlier and had been rewarded with the sounds of them gobbling them up.

"The wardens are here." Carter waved at the main hall. "They caught the poachers, so that's a small comfort. Katherine and Tamaya are filling them in on all the recent drama. You mentioned earlier that you wanted to speak to them too?"

"Did I?" Kea asked. "I seem to say things these days without thinking them through properly. I must be getting old. I don't think I can help them with anything else."

"Well, you missed the good part." Carter grinned, his eyes filled with mischief.

"Which was?"

"When we told them it was the rover, in the jeep, with the poison."

Kea smirked. "I doubt Gwen will be allowed to have knitting needles in prison…although it's sad to think about Sock behind bars."

"On the bright side, now the system's up again, we found some more meerkats that escaped. They should be able to help Hazel raise those pups."

"A happy ending at last? We need more of those. Speaking of, how'd you leave things with Tshepo?"

Carter sat on the step below her. "I left an open invitation for him to visit in San Diego. First, though he's got to decide if he's going to have a difficult conversation with his wife. Or not. That's up to him. We are, however, going to make sure to hand over that photo of the poachers. Hopefully they can shut that down." He pointed to the glass of wine in her hands. "Not mixing that with sleeping pills, I hope?"

"I'm going to try not to." She rubbed the back of her neck. "I'm not usually this much of a mess, you know. Just having a bit of a life crisis right now."

Carter pursed his lips. "How bad is it?"

Kea wanted to say everything, lay it all out, but the truth was too much. It had already scared away everyone she cared about.

I'm worried that in Iceland I had to kill to survive and I'm okay with it. In fact, I enjoyed it.

I dread falling asleep because of the nightmares that wait for me there.

My father passed away last year, and I wasn't there because I was doing fieldwork. I want to not care because he stopped speaking to me when I was twenty-two and he found out I was bi-sexual, but his absence left a hole in my being.

I have no place to live because I took too much sleep medicine, hallucinated, and then nearly stabbed my girlfriend's teenage son. She broke up with me and kicked me out of our home.

Pick one, her therapist had advised.

Just start with one, and let people in, slowly. "Would you believe, I just had a job offer?" Kea thought back to Amirah's video chat.

"More glaciers?"

"No. I mean, possibly. It was a great deal of money. I think I might even take it."

Carter pursed his lips. "It's not in the detective business, I hope?"

Kea laughed. "God no. I think I'm fairly terrible at that. However, if I get a new job, I'll need to go apartment hunting. Living in my office is a great commute, but the square footage leaves a lot to be desired." The small matter of the break-in at the university still nagged at her, but she was beginning to have an idea of how to handle it. "On the plus side, I'm due to go back to Iceland in a couple of months, and tents are nearly rent-free. Ever been to Iceland?"

Carter frowned in mock frustration. "I've never been, but my cousins from South America recently went to Italy. Its beauty made them cry. You could say, they were 'Venice wailin'."

Kea raised her glass to the sky in a toast.

"To Tristan." They whispered together.

After a moment, she asked, "Know anything about glaciers?"

Carter shrugged. "As it snow happens, I do…"

"Icy what you did there."

"Should we stop now?"

"Yes please."

Dr. Kea Wright will return in:

Murder on Masaya

Acknowledgements

Thanks to the regulars:
Tracy, Suzanne, Dan, Angelo, Tiffany, Jess, Lisa, Julie & Andy &
Jack, Morgan, Ben, Michaela & Kevin, Anita & JP, Mom, Maeghan,
Aimee, Carsten, and Scott.

Many thanks to the Village of Potsdam.
Its beautiful toilet gardens make it a premier destination for anyone
visiting Upstate New York.

Disclaimer

Although there are several amazing resorts in Botswana, Mackenzie Camp does not exist. Although parts of the Kalahari do experience a great deal of annual rainfall, the size of the storm and flood channels described in this work were exaggerated for dramatic effect.

Made in the USA
Las Vegas, NV
04 April 2022

46880086R10097